DAMAGED

Special Agent Maggie O'Dell thought she had seen it all in her career. Amidst the killers, psychos and criminals she has hunted, she's delved into the darkest, most shockingly evil recesses of the human mind. But when a cool box filled with individually wrapped body parts washes up on the shore of Florida's Pensacola Beach, even Maggie is appalled. While across the state people brace themselves against a monster hurricane, Maggie must track down a determined killer – before he strikes again.

DAMAGED

DAMAGED

by

Alex Kava

Magna Large Print Books
Long Preston, North Yorkshire,
BD23 4ND, England.

British Library Cataloguing in Publication Data.

Kava, Alex
    Damaged.

    A catalogue record of this book is
    available from the British Library

    ISBN   978-0-7505-3484-0

First published in Great Britain in 2010 by Sphere

Copyright © S. M. Kava 2010

Maps designed by Jeffrey L. Ward

Cover illustration © Jon Browning by arrangement with
Arcangel Images

The moral right of the author has been asserted

Published in Large Print 2011 by arrangement with
Little, Brown Book Group

Magna Large Print is an imprint of Library Magna Books Ltd.

Printed and bound in Great Britain by
T.J. (International) Ltd., Cornwall, PL28 8RW

TO PHYLLIS GRANN,
for your patience, your perseverance,
and your wisdom.
Here's to new beginnings.

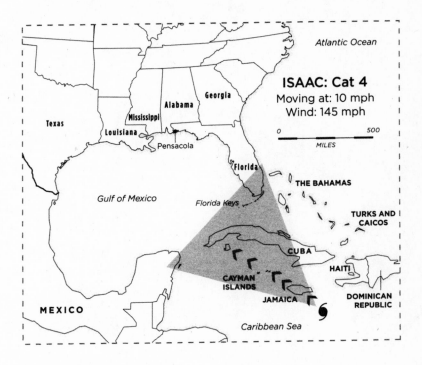

ONE

PENSACOLA BAY
PENSACOLA, FLORIDA

Elizabeth Bailey didn't like what she saw. Even now, after their H-65 helicopter came down into a hover less than two hundred feet above the rolling Gulf, the object in the water still looked like a container and certainly not a capsized boat. There were no thrashing arms or legs. No bobbing heads. No one needing to be rescued, as far as she could see. Yet Lieutenant Commander Wilson, their aircrew pilot, insisted they check it out. What he really meant was that Liz would check it out.

A Coast Guard veteran at only twenty-seven years old, AST3 Liz Bailey knew she had chalked up more rescues in two days over New Orleans after Hurricane Katrina than Wilson had in his entire two-year career. Liz had dropped onto rickety apartment balconies, scraped her knees on wind-battered roofs, and waded through debris-filled water that smelled of raw sewage.

She dared not mention any of this. It didn't matter how many search and rescues she'd performed, because at the moment she was the newbie at Air Station Mobile, and she'd need to prove herself all over again. To add insult to injury, within her first week someone had decorated the women's locker room by plastering downloaded photos of her from a 2005 issue of *People* magazine. Her superiors insisted that the feature article would be good PR for the Coast Guard, especially when other military and government agencies were taking a beating over their response to Katrina. But in an organization where attention to individual and ego could jeopardize team missions, her unwanted notoriety threatened to be the kiss of death for her career. Four years later, it still followed her around like a curse.

By comparison, what Wilson was asking probably seemed tame. So what if the floating container might be a fisherman's cooler washed overboard? What was the harm in checking it out? Except that rescue swimmers were trained to risk their lives in order to save other lives, not to retrieve inanimate objects. In fact, there was an unwritten rule about it. After several swimmers who were asked to haul up bales of drugs tested positive for drug use, apparently from their intimate contact in the water, it was decided the risk to the rescue team was too great. Wilson must have missed that memo.

Besides, rescue swimmers could also elect

not to deploy. In other words, she could tell Lieutenant Commander less-than-a-thousand-flight-hours Wilson that 'hell no,' she wasn't jumping into the rough waters for some fisherman's discarded catch of the day.

Wilson turned in his seat to look at her. From the tilt of his square chin he reminded her of a boxer daring a punch. The glint in his eyes pinned her down, his helmet's visor slid up for greater impact. He didn't need to say out loud what his body language said for him: 'So, Bailey, are you a prima donna or are you a team player?'

Liz wasn't stupid. She knew that as one of less than a dozen women rescue swimmers, she was a rare breed. She was used to having to constantly prove herself. She recognized the stakes in the water as well as those in the helicopter. These were the men she'd have to trust to pull her back up when she dangled by a cable seventy feet below, out in the open, over angry seas, sometimes spinning in the wind.

Liz had learned early on that she was expected to perform a number of complicated balancing acts. While it was necessary to be fiercely independent and capable of working alone, she also understood what the vulnerabilities were. Her life was ultimately in the hands of the crew above. Today and next week and the week after next, it would be these guys. And until they felt like she had truly proven herself, she would continue to be *the* rescue swimmer' instead of *our* rescue swimmer.'

Liz kept her hesitation to herself, avoided Wilson's eyes, and pretended to be more interested in checking out the water below. She simply listened. Inside her helmet, via the ICS (internal communication system), Wilson started relaying their strategy, telling his co-pilot, Lieutenant Junior Grade Tommy Ellis, and their flight mechanic, AST3 Pete Kesnick, to prepare for a direct deployment using the RS (rescue swimmer) and the basket. He was already reducing their position from two hundred feet to eighty feet.

'Might just be an empty fishing cooler,' Kesnick said.

Liz watched him out of the corner of her eyes. Kesnick didn't like this, either. The senior member of the aircrew, Kesnick had a tanned weathered face with crinkle lines at his eyes and mouth that never changed, never telegraphed whether he was angry or pleased.

'Or it might be cocaine,' Ellis countered. 'They found fifty kilos washed ashore someplace in Texas.'

'McFaddin Beach,' Wilson filled in. 'Sealed and wrapped in thick plastic. Someone missed a drop-off or panicked and tossed it. Could be what we have here.'

16

'Then shouldn't we radio it in and leave it for a cutter to pick up?' Kesnick said as he glanced at Liz. She could tell he was trying to let her know that he'd back her if she elected not to deploy.

Wilson noticed the glance. 'It's up to you, Bailey. What do you want to do?'

She still didn't meet his eyes, didn't want to give him the satisfaction of seeing even a hint of her reluctance.

'We should use the medevac board instead of the basket,' she said. 'It'll be easier to slide it under the container and strap it down.'

Knowing he was surprised by her response, she simply removed her flight helmet, cutting off communication. If Ellis or Kesnick had something to say about her, she dared them to say it after her attempt at nonchalance.

She fingered strands of her hair back under her surf cap and strapped on her lightweight Seda helmet. She attached the gunner's belt to her harness, positioned the quick strop over her shoulders, made sure to keep the friction slide close to the hoist hook. Finished, she moved to the door of the helicopter, squatted in position, and waited for Kesnick's signal.

She couldn't avoid looking at him. They had done this routine at least half a dozen times since she started at the air station. She suspected that Pete Kesnick treated her no differently than he had been treating rescue swimmers for the last fifteen years of his career as a Coastie flight mechanic and hoist operator. Even now, he didn't second-guess her, though his steel-blue eyes studied her a second longer than usual before he flipped down his visor.

He tapped her on the chest, the signal for 'ready' – two gloved fingers practically at her collarbone. Probably not the same tap he used with male rescue swimmers. Liz didn't mind. It was a small thing, done out of respect more than anything else.

She released the gunner's belt, gave Kesnick a thumbs-up to tell him she was ready. She maintained control over the quick strop as he hoisted her clear of the deck. Then he stopped. Liz readjusted herself as the cable pulled tight. She turned and gave Kesnick another thumbs-up and descended into the rolling waters.

Without a survivor in the water Liz quickly assessed the situation. The container was huge. By Liz's estimates, at least forty inches long and twenty inches wide and deep. She recognized the battered white stainless steel as a commercial-grade marine cooler. A frayed tie-down floated from its handle bracket. Frayed, not cut. So maybe its owner hadn't intended to ditch it, after all. She grabbed the tie-down, which was made of bright yellow-and-blue strands twisted into a half-inch-thick rope, and looped it through her harness to keep the cooler from bobbing away in the rotor wash of the helicopter.

She signaled Kesnick: her left arm raised, her right arm crossing over her head and touching her left elbow. She was ready for them to deploy the medevac board.

The bobbing container fought against her, pushing and pulling with each wave, not able to go any farther than the rope attached to her belt allowed. It took two attempts but within fifteen minutes Liz had the fishing cooler attached to the medevac board. She cinched the restraints tight, hooked it to the cable, and raised her arm again, giving a thumbs-up.

No records broken, but by the time Kesnick hoisted her back into the helicopter, she could tell her crew was pleased. Not impressed, but pleased. It was a small step.

Lieutenant Commander Wilson still looked impatient. Liz barely caught her breath, but yanked off her Seda helmet, exchanging it for her flight helmet with the communications gear inside. She caught Wilson in the middle of instructing Kesnick to open the latch.

'Shouldn't we wait?' Kesnick tried being the diplomat.

'It's not locked. Just take a peek.'

Liz slid out of the way and to the side of the cabin, unbuckling the rest of her gear. She didn't want any part of this. As far as she was concerned, her job was finished.

Kesnick paused and at first she thought he would refuse. He moved to her side and pushed back his visor, avoiding her eyes. The child-safety latch slid back without effort but he had to use the palm of his hand to shove the snap lock free. Liz saw him draw in a deep breath before he flung open the lid.

The first thing Liz noticed was the fish-measuring ruler molded into the lid. It seemed an odd thing to notice but later it would stick in her mind. A fetid smell escaped but it wasn't rotten fish. More like opening a Dumpster.

Inside she could see what looked like thick plastic wrap encasing several oblong objects, one large and four smaller. Not the square bundles that might be cocaine.

'Well?' Wilson asked, trying to glance over his shoulder.

Kesnick poked at one of the smaller bundles with a gloved finger. It flipped over. The plastic was more transparent on this side and suddenly the content was unmistakable.

His eyes met Liz's and now the ever calm, poker-faced Kesnick looked panicked.

'I think it's a foot,' he said.

'What?'

'I think it's a goddamn human foot.'

TWO

NEWBURGH HEIGHTS, VIRGINIA

Maggie O'Dell peeled off her blouse without undoing the buttons, popping one before it came off. Didn't matter. The blouse was a goner. Even the best cleaners couldn't take out this much blood.

She folded the shirt into a wad and dropped it into her bathroom sink. Something wet was stuck to her neck. She grabbed at it, threw it in the sink.

Pink. Like clotted cheese.

She'd been so close. Too close when the fatal shot came. Impossible to get out of the way.

She swatted at her neck and yanked at her hair, expecting more pieces. Her fingers got stuck in sweaty tangles, damp, sticky. But, thank God, no more chunks.

They hadn't expected the killer to still be there. The warehouse appeared empty, only remnants of his torture chamber remained, just as Maggie had predicted. Why the hell had he stayed? Or had he come back? To watch.

Maggie's boss, Assistant Director Raymond Kunze, had made the fatal shot. And afterward he was already taking it out on Maggie, as if it were her fault, as if she had forced his hand. But there was no way she could have known that the killer was there, hiding in the shadows. No profiler could have predicted that. Kunze couldn't possibly hold her accountable, and yet she knew he would do exactly *that*.

Harvey, her white Lab, grabbed one of her discarded, muddy shoes. Rather than taking it to play he dropped to his belly and started whining, a low guttural moan that tugged at Maggie's heart.

'Come on and drop it, Harvey,' she ordered, but instead of scolding, she said it quietly, gently.

He could smell the blood on her, was already concerned. But the shoe plopped out of his mouth.

'Sorry, big guy.'

Maggie swiped the shoe up and placed it in the sink with her soiled blouse. Then she knelt down beside Harvey, petting him. She wanted to hug him but there was still too much blood on her.

'Wait for me outside, buddy,' she said, leading him out of the huge master bathroom and into her bedroom, telling him to sit where he could see her through the doorway. She scratched behind his ears until he relaxed, waiting for his sigh and his collapse into lay-down position.

The smell of blood still panicked him. She hated the reminder. With it came the memory of that day she found him, bleeding and cowering under his first owner's bed, right in the middle of his own bloody ordeal. The dog had fought hard and still had been unsuccessful in protecting his mistress, who had been taken from her house and later murdered.

'I'm okay,' she reassured him, as she dared to take a good look at herself in the mirror to see if what she said was true.

It wasn't so bad. She'd been through worse. And at least this time it wasn't her own blood.

Her tangled, dark-auburn hair almost reached her shoulders. She needed to get it trimmed. What a thing to think about. Her eyes were bloodshot but it had nothing to do with this incident. She hadn't been able to sleep through the night for months now, waking every hour on the hour as if some alarm in her head triggered it. The sleep deprivation was bound to catch up with her.

She had tried all the recommended remedies. An evening run to exhaust her body. No exercise at all after seven. Soaking in a warm bath. Drinking a glass of wine. When wine didn't work, warm milk. She tried reciting meditation chants. Cutting out caffeine. Reading. Listening to CDs of nature sounds.

Using new therapeutic pillows. Lighting candles with soothing aromas. Even a little Scotch in the warm milk.

Nothing worked.

She hadn't resorted to sleep meds ... yet. As an FBI special agent and profiler she received phone calls in the middle of the night or the early morning hours that sometimes made it necessary for her to rush to a crime scene. Most of the meds – the good ones – required eight hours of uninterrupted sleep time. Who had that? Certainly not an agent.

She took a long, hot shower, gently washing. No scrubbing, though that was her first inclination. She avoided watching the drain and what went down. She left her hair damp. Put on a clean, loose-fitting pair of athletic shorts and her University of Virginia T-shirt. After bagging up her clothes – at least those that couldn't be salvaged – and tossing them in the garbage, Maggie retreated to the main room. Harvey followed close behind.

She turned on the big-screen TV, pocketing the remote and continuing on to the kitchen. The fifty-six-inch plasma had been a splurge for someone who watched little television, but she justified it by having college-football parties on Saturdays in the fall. And then there were the evenings of pizza, beer, and classic movies with Ben. Colonel Benjamin

Platt had become a close ... friend.

That was all for now, or so they had decided. Okay, so they hadn't really even talked about it. Things were at a comfortable level. She liked talking to him as much as she liked the silence of being with him. Sometimes when they sat in her backyard watching Harvey and Ben's dog, Digger, play, Maggie caught herself thinking, 'This could be a family.' The four of them seemed to fill voids in each other's lives.

Yes, comfortable. She liked that. Except that lately she felt an annoying tingle every time he touched her. That's when she reminded herself that both their lives were already complicated and their personal baggage sometimes untenable. Their schedules constantly conflicted. Especially the last three to four months.

So 'friends' was a comfortable place to be for now, though decided by default rather than consensus. Still, she caught herself checking her cell phone: waiting, expecting, hoping for a message from him. She hadn't seen him since he'd spent two weeks in Afghanistan. Only short phone conversations or text messages.

Now he was gone again. Somewhere in Florida. She wasn't used to them not being able to share. That was one of the things that had brought them closer, talking about their various cases: hers usually profiling a killer; his identifying or controlling some infectious disease. A couple of times they had worked on a case together when the FBI and USAMRIID (United States Army Medical Research Institute of Infectious Diseases – pronounced U-SAM-RID) were both involved. But Afghanistan and this trip were, in Ben's words, 'classified missions' in 'undisclosed locations.' In Maggie's mind, she added 'dangerous.'

She fed Harvey while tossing a salad for herself and listening to 'breaking news' at the top of the hour:

'Gas prices are up and will continue to soar because of the tropical storms and hurricanes that have ravaged the Gulf this summer. And another one, Hurricane Isaac is predicted to sweep across Jamaica tonight. The category-4 storm with sustained winds of 145 miles per hour is expected to pick up steam when it enters the Gulf in the next couple of days.'

Her cell phone rang and she jumped, startled enough to spill salad dressing on the counter. Okay, so having a killer's blood and brains splattered all over her had unnerved her more than she was willing to admit.

She grabbed for the phone. Checked the number, disappointed that she didn't recognize it.

'This is Maggie O'Dell.'

'Hey, *cherie,*' a smooth, baritone voice said. There was only one person who got away

26

with using that New Orleans charm on her.

'Hello, Charlie. And to what do I owe this pleasure?'

Maggie and Charlie Wurth had spent last Thanksgiving weekend sorting through a bombing at Mall of America and trying to prevent another before the weekend was over. In a case where she couldn't even trust her new boss, AD Raymond Kunze, Charlie Wurth had been a godsend. For six months now the deputy director of the Department of Homeland Security (DHS) had been trying to woo her over to his side of the fence at the Justice Department.

'I'm headed on a road trip,' Charlie continued. 'And I know you won't be able to say no to joining me. Think sunny Florida. Emerald-green waters. Sugar-white sands.'

Every once in a while Charlie Wurth called just to dangle another of his outrageous proposals. It had become a game with them. She couldn't remember why she hadn't entertained the idea of leaving the FBI and working for DHS. She swiped her fingers through her hair, thinking about the blood and brain matter from earlier. Maybe she should consider a switch.

'Sounds wonderful.' Maggie played along. 'What's the catch?'

'Just a small one. It appears we most likely will be in the projected path of Hurricane Isaac.'

'Tell me again why I'd be interested in going along?'

'Actually, you'd be doing me a big favor.' Charlie's voice turned serious. 'I was already on my way down because of the hurricane. Got a bit of a distraction, though. Coast Guard found a fishing cooler in the Gulf.'

He left a pause inviting her to finish.

'Let me guess. It wasn't filled with fish.'

'Exactly. Local law enforcement has its hands full with hurricane preps. Coast Guard makes it DHS, but I'm thinking the assortment of body parts throws it over to FBI. I just checked with AD Kunze to see if I can borrow you.'

'You talked to Kunze? Today?'

'Yep. Just a few minutes ago. He seemed to think it'd be a good idea.'

She wasn't surprised that her boss wanted to send her into the eye of a hurricane.

THREE

NAVAL AIR STATION (NAS) PENSACOLA, FLORIDA

Colonel Benjamin Platt didn't recognize this part of the base, though he'd been here once before. Usually he was in and out of these places too quickly to become familiar with any of them.

'It's gorgeous,' he said, looking out at Pensacola Bay.

His escort, Captain Carl Ganz, seemed caught off guard by the comment, turning around to see just what Platt was pointing out. Their driver slowed as if to assist his captain's view.

'Oh yes, definitely. Guess we take it for granted,' Captain Ganz said. 'Pensacola is one of the prettiest places I've been stationed. Just getting back from Kabul, I'm sure this looks especially gorgeous.'

'You're right about that.'

'How was it?'

'The trip?'

'Afghanistan.'

'The dust never lets up. Still feel like my lungs haven't cleared.'

'I remember. I was part of a medevac team in 2005,' Captain Ganz told Platt.

'I didn't realize that.'

'Summer 2005. We lost one of our SEALs. A four-member reconnaissance contingent came under attack. Then a helicopter carrying sixteen soldiers flew in as a reinforcement but was shot down.' Ganz kept his eyes on the water in the bay. 'All aboard died. As did the ground crew.'

Platt let out a breath and shook his head. 'That's not a good day.'

'You were there back then, too, weren't you?'

'Earlier. Actually, the first months of the war,' Platt said. 'I was part of the team trying to protect our guys from biological or chemical weapons. Ended up cutting and suturing more than anything else.'

'So has it changed?'

'The war?'

'Afghanistan.'

Platt paused and studied Captain Ganz. He was a little older than Platt, maybe forty, with a boyish face, although his hair had prematurely turned gray. This was the first time the two men had met in person. Past correspondences had been via e-mail and phone calls. Platt was a medical doctor and director of infectious diseases at Fort Detrick's USAMRIID and charged with preventing, inoculating, and containing some of the deadliest diseases ever known. Ganz, also a physician, ran a medical program for the navy that oversaw the surgical needs of wounded soldiers.

'Sadly, no,' Platt finally answered, deciding he could be honest with Ganz. 'Reminded me too much of those early days. Seems like we're chasing our tails. Only now we're doing it with our hands tied behind our backs.'

Platt rubbed a thumb and forefinger over his eyes, trying to wipe out the fatigue. He still felt jet-lagged from his flight. He hadn't been back home even forty-eight hours when he got the call from Captain Ganz.

'Tell me about this mystery virus.' Platt decided he'd just as well cut to the chase.

'We've isolated and quarantined every soldier we think may have come in contact with the first cases, the ones that are now breaking. Until we know what it is, I figured it's better to be safe than sorry.'

'Absolutely. What are the symptoms?'

'That's just it. There are very few. At least, in the beginning. Initially there's excruciating pain at the surgical site, which is not unusual with most of these surgeries. We're talking multiple fractures, deep-tissue wounds with bone exposed.' He paused as several planes took off overhead, drowning out all sound. 'We're starting to move aircraft out of the path of this next hurricane.'

'I thought it's predicted to hit farther west,

maybe New Orleans.'

'Media is always looking at New Orleans,' Ganz shrugged. 'Better story I guess. But some of the best in the weather business are telling us it's coming here. Just hope we're on the left side of it and not the right. That's why the admiral's nervous. That's why I told him I needed to call you in. I told him, if Platt can't figure this out, no one can.'

'Not sure I can live up to that.'

'Yes, you can. You will. You have to.'

'Pain at the site,' Platt prodded him to continue, wanting to keep focused before the fatigue derailed him. 'What about the med packs left at the site?'

'That's what we thought with the first cases. We removed the packs and that seemed to alleviate the pain, but only temporarily.'

'Infection?'

'Surgical sites show no swelling. Patients have no fever. Although they report feeling very hot and sometimes sweat profusely. They complain about upset stomachs. Some vomiting. Headaches. And yet all vital signs are good. Blood pressure, heart rate ... all normal. Here we are.' Captain Ganz stopped as his driver pulled up to a side entrance of a brick two-story building.

The steel door was reinforced. A security keypad blinked red, its digital message flashed C CLASS I.

Ganz punched in a number then pressed

his thumb on the screen. Locks clicked open: one, two, three of them. Inside was a small lobby, but Ganz took Platt down the first hallway to the right. The corridor was narrow and the two men walked shoulder to shoulder.

'The admiral wants me to evacuate these soldiers. Move them inland to the Naval Hospital instead of keeping them here right on the bay. But, as you know, moving them presents all kinds of problems.'

Finally they arrived at another door, another security keypad. Ganz went through the same process again, but when the locks clicked this time he pulled the door open just a few inches and stopped, turning back to look Platt in the eyes.

'Within a week, four, five days, the blood pressure plunges. The heart starts racing. It's like the body is struggling to get oxygen. They slip into a coma. Organs rapidly begin to shut down. There's been nothing we can do. I've lost two so far. Just yesterday. I don't want the rest of these soldiers to see the same end.'

'I understand. Let's see what we can do.'

Ganz nodded, opened the door, and walked into a small glass-encased room that overlooked an area as big as a gymnasium, only it was sectioned and partitioned off, each section encased in a plastic tent with sterile walls that sprouted tubes and cords, monitors and computer screens.

Platt sucked in his breath to prevent a gasp. There had to be more than a hundred hospital beds filling the space. More than a hundred beds with more than a hundred soldiers.

FOUR

PENSACOLA BEACH

Liz Bailey would have rather stayed out in the Gulf and be battered by the waves and the wind. But they were grounded for the rest of their shift and for the last five hours had been battered by the sheriff of Escambia County, the director of the Santa Rosa Island Authority, the commander of Air Station Pensacola, a federal investigator from the Department of Homeland Security, and the deputy director of DHS via speakerphone.

It was crazy and Liz couldn't help wondering if they might have gotten off easier if they had never looked inside the cooler. If only they'd just handed it over and headed back out. Too many of the questions seemed more about containment of information rather than gathering the facts.

'Who else have you told?' the sheriff wanted

to know.

'We followed proper procedure for finding human remains at sea.' Lieutenant Commander Wilson no longer bothered to hide his impatience. Keeping a cool head was a skill Wilson hadn't learned yet.

Liz wondered if he was sorry that he'd asked Kesnick to open the cooler. Seeing him defensive and irritated by the consequences of his actions was almost worth the detainment. Almost.

Earlier, the look on Wilson's face had convinced Liz that their pilot had never seen a severed body part before. At first she thought Wilson didn't believe Kesnick. But she saw his eyes and glimpsed what looked like fear – maybe even shock. With his visor pushed back to get a better look at the contents inside that cooler, there was no hiding his expression. At least not from Liz, who had been in a position in the helicopter to see it, to catch it straight on. Normally it may have garnered sympathy. Instead it simply reinforced her lack of respect for the guy.

Finally dismissed for the day, the four of them wandered out into the sunlight.

'Beer's on me,' Wilson announced. 'It's early. We can get a good seat on the Tiki Bar's deck. Watch some bikini babes.'

Someone cleared his throat. Liz didn't look to see who.

'Oh, come on,' Wilson said. 'Bailey doesn't

mind. Not if she's one of us.'

Always the edge, the challenge, putting it back onto Liz.

'Actually, it sounds like a good idea,' she said, putting on her sunglasses, still without looking at any of them and not slowing her pace.

'Only if we can get a couple of hot dogs.' Tommy Ellis was always hungry.

'Geez, Ellis. Can you stop thinking about your stomach? We'll get them later,' Wilson insisted.

'What if the hot-dog man isn't there later?'

'He'll be there,' Liz told them, now leading the way to the Tiki Bar. 'And he'll probably talk us into going out again for another beer with him.'

'Yeah, how can you be so sure?' Ellis demanded.

'Because the hot-dog man is my dad.'

FIVE

NEWBURGH HEIGHTS, VIRGINIA

Maggie O'Dell downloaded and printed the copies Wurth had forwarded to her. The photos and initial documents from the Escambia County Sheriff's Department reminded her that she'd want to take her own photos. She'd be able to decipher only the basics from these shots.

One photo showed an assortment of odd-shaped packages wrapped in plastic and stuffed inside an oversize cooler. The close-ups displayed the individual packages lined up on a concrete floor used for staging. What she could see beyond the plastic wrap looked more like cuts of meat from a butcher shop than parts of a human body.

She asked Wurth if they could wait until her arrival before unwrapping the packages. He told her it was probably too late.

'Doubtful. You know how that goes, O'Dell. Curiosity gets the best of even law enforcement.' But then he added, 'I'll see what I can do.'

Now Maggie sat cross-legged in the middle of her living-room floor, scattered photos on one side, Harvey on the other. His sleeping head filled her lap. She kept the TV on the Weather Channel. Initially the TV just provided background noise, but she found the weather coverage drawing her attention. She was learning about hurricanes, something that might come in handy in the following week.

Maggie found it interesting that the Saffir-Simpson Hurricane Wind Scale, though measured by sustained winds, was also based on the level of damage those winds were capable of causing. A category-3 storm produced sustained winds of 111 to 130 miles per hour and could cause 'extensive' damage; a category 4, 131 to 155 mile per hour winds and 'devastating' damage; a category 5, 156 miles per hour and greater winds with 'catastrophic' damage.

One hundred and forty mile per hour winds were not something Maggie could relate to. Damage, however, was something she could.

Hurricane Isaac had already killed sixty people across the Caribbean. Within several hours it had gone from 145 mile per hour winds to 150. The storm was expected to hit Grand Cayman in a few hours. One million Cubans were said to have evacuated in anticipation of the monster hitting there on Sunday. Moving at only ten miles per hour, the hurricane was expected to enter the Gulf by Monday.

On every projected path Maggie had seen in the last several hours, Pensacola, Florida, was smack-dab in the middle. Charlie Wurth hadn't been kidding when he told her they would be driving down into the eye of a hurricane. Consequently, there were no available flights to Pensacola. Tomorrow morning she was booked to fly to Atlanta, where Charlie would pick her up and they would drive five hours to the Florida Panhandle. When she asked him what he was doing in Atlanta – his home was in New Orleans and his office in Washington, D.C. – he simply said, 'Don't ask.'

Wurth still had difficulty acting like a federal government employee. He came to the position of assistant deputy director of Homeland Security after impressing the right people with his tough but fair investigation of federal waste and corruption in the wake of Hurricane Katrina. But Wurth, like Maggie, probably would never get used to the bureaucracy that came with the job.

Maggie knew she should be packing. She kept a bag with the essentials. She just needed to add to it. What did one pack for hurricane weather? Sensible shoes, no doubt. Her friend Gwen Patterson was always telling Maggie that she didn't have the appropriate respect for shoes.

She glanced at the time. She'd need to call Gwen. She'd do that later. The foray with today's killer was still too fresh in her mind and on her skin. Her friend the psychiatrist had a knack for reading between the lines, weighing pauses, and detecting even the slightest of cracks in Maggie's composure. An occupational hazard, Gwen always said, and Maggie understood all too well.

The two women had met when Maggie was a forensic fellow at Quantico and Gwen a private consultant to the Behavioral Science Unit. Seventeen years Maggie's senior, Dr.

Gwen Patterson had the tendency to overlap maternal instincts into their friendship. Maggie didn't mind. Gwen was her one constant. It was Gwen who was always there by Maggie's side. It was Gwen propping her up during her long, drawn-out divorce; setting up vigil alongside Maggie's hospital bed after a killer had trapped her in a freezer to die; sitting outside an isolation ward at Fort Detrick when Maggie'd been exposed to Ebola; and most recently Gwen was again by her side at Arlington National Cemetery when Maggie paid her last respects at her mentor's gravesite.

Yet there were days like today when Maggie didn't want to confront her own vulnerabilities. Nor did she want her friend worrying. Maggie knew her insomnia was not just the inability to fall asleep. It was the nightmares that jolted her awake. Visions of her brother Patrick handcuffed to a suitcase bomb. The image of her mentor and boss lying in a hospital bed, his skeletal body invaded with tubes and needles. Herself trapped inside an ice coffin. A takeout container left on the counter of a truck stop, seeping blood. Rows and rows of Mason jars filled with floating body parts.

The problem was that those nightmare images were not the creation of an overactive or fatigued imagination but, rather, were memories, snapshots of very real ex-

40

periences. The compartments Maggie had spent years carefully constructing in her mind – the places where she locked away the horrific snapshots – had started to leak. Just like Gwen had predicted.

'One of these days,' her wise friend had warned, 'you're going to need to deal with the things you've seen and done, what's been done to you. You can't tuck them away forever.'

The cell phone startled both Maggie and Harvey this time. She patted him as she reached across his body to retrieve the phone. She wouldn't have been surprised to hear Gwen's voice.

'Maggie O'Dell.'

'Hey.'

Close. It was Gwen's boyfriend, R. J. Tully, who happened to be Maggie's partner. That was before the FBI buckled down on costs. Now they found themselves working singularly and assigned to very few of the same cases. However, Tully had been one of the contingency there today at the warehouse, one of half a dozen agents who witnessed Kunze's kill shot.

'Thought I'd check to see if you're okay.'

'I'm fine.' Too quick. She bit down on her lower lip. Would Tully call her on it? Gwen would. Before he had a chance to respond, she tried to change the subject. 'I was just about to call Emma.'

41

'Emma?' Tully sounded like he didn't recognize his daughter's name.

'To stay with Harvey. I need to leave to-morrow morning. Early. Charlie Wurth has a case in Florida he wants me to check out. Is Emma home?'

Too long of a pause. He knew what she was up to. He was a profiler, too. But would he let her get away with it? Gwen wouldn't.

'She hasn't left for college yet, has she?' Maggie asked the question only to fill the silence. She knew the girl was dragging her feet about going.

'No. Not until late next week. She's not here right now, but I'm sure she'll be okay about staying with Harvey. Text her instead of calling. You'll get an immediate response.' Another pause. 'Does AD Kunze know about this trip?'

'Of course, he does.' She hated that it came out with an edge. 'Wurth checked it out with him.' She didn't add that Kunze thought it was a good idea. Tully would add it on his own. He had faced the wrath of Kunze last fall when their new boss put Tully on suspension. 'It's probably not a big deal,' Maggie jumped in again. 'Some body parts found in a cooler off the coast.'

'More body parts.' She could hear Tully laugh. 'Sounds like you're becoming an expert on killers who chop up their victims.'

She would have laughed, too, if it wasn't

so close to being true. Then, without regard to all the work she had done to change the subject, Maggie heard herself say, 'Do me a favor, don't tell Gwen about today, okay?'

'Not a problem.' This time there had been no pause, no hesitation. A partner backing up another partner. 'Let me know if I can help. With the case,' he added, allowing her cover.

SIX

HILTON PENSACOLA BEACH GULF FRONT

Scott Larsen sipped his draft beer and waited for the man he'd secretly nicknamed 'the Death Salesman.' It was sort of a term of endearment, one colleague to another. After all, Scott didn't mind that some people – including his own wife – sometimes called him a death merchant. Sounded sexier than funeral director or even mortician.

He watched the back door to the hotel from the deck bar. This was the first time they were meeting outside of Scott's office. Scott was good at his job, good at being the professional. He didn't do casual or social very well, and in his line of work you never

43

mixed business with pleasure so it worked just fine.

The cute, blond bartender had already given him a refill and his head was beginning to feel a bit fuzzy. He'd never been good at holding his liquor, even beer, though he was pretty good at pretending. As soon as the buzz began, he slowed down his speech and carefully measured his words.

His wife, Trish, claimed he was too good at pretending. But then he'd had a lot of practice. That was, after all, what the funeral business was all about, wasn't it? Pretend the deceased is at peace. Pretend he's gone on to a better place. Pretend that you care.

Scott glanced at his wristwatch and turned to look back at the water. He tried not to stare at any of the young bikinied bodies though the beach was filled with them this early on a Saturday evening. He was a married man now, or at least he could use that as an excuse. He stunk at flirting, too. He could be so charming when it came to widows, holding their hands and letting them sob on his shoulder. But put him in a room full of beautiful, sexy women and he choked. Had no clue what to do or what to talk about. His palms got sweaty, his tongue swelled in his mouth. Couldn't even fake his way around. It was a wonder he ever snagged Trish. He was lucky and grateful and he tried never to forget that.

He started to turn back around to watch the hotel door when he noticed a guy walking up the beach with a confident, relaxed stride, deck shoes in one hand and the other casually slipped into the pocket of his long khaki shorts. The hem of his pink button-down shirt flapped in the breeze. He wasn't stunningly handsome and yet that confident stride turned some heads. The guy looked like he had stepped off the cover of GQ and nothing like a death salesman. In fact, it took a minute or two before Scott recognized him. He certainly hadn't expected him to come walking up the beach.

Scott waved at him then felt ridiculous when he didn't receive an acknowledgment. Instead, the guy simply strolled through the crowd of bikinis and made his way to the barstool next to Scott without even a nod or glance. He was always so cool.

'What do you have for Scotch, single malt?' he asked the cute bartender, who was already in front of him by the time he settled in his seat.

'Sorry, no single malts and the best blend I've got is Johnnie Walker.'

'Blue Label?'

Scott watched the bartender smile with what looked like admiration.

'No, again, sorry. Black Label's best I can do.'

'That's perfect,' he told her, as if that was

exactly what he wanted all along. Then he turned to Scott. 'Join me?'

The attention caught Scott off guard, like a spectator suddenly pulled onto the playing field. The bartender, probably thinking Scott was some total stranger, now seemed even more impressed and she was waiting for Scott's response.

'Sure. Thanks,' he managed as casually as he could.

'On the rocks for both of you?' she asked.

'Yeah, that'd be great,' Scott told her, pretending it was his preference when he couldn't remember if he'd ever had Scotch before.

'Neat, for me.'

Another smile from the bartender that almost made Scott want to change his order.

'This place was a great choice, Scott,' the Death Salesman said, and Scott immediately relaxed and felt a rush ... of what? It was silly but there really was something about this guy that made you want to please him.

That's when Scott realized he needed to calm his buzz down a notch so that he didn't slip and call him by the nickname in his head. Scott had wondered if Joe Black was his real name from the first time he introduced himself. That was, after all, the name of a movie character. This guy didn't look at all like Brad Pitt, but he certainly had that same charm and confidence. And the irony, if it was not his real name, only garnered more admiration from Scott. Joe Black, the character in the movie, was actually death masquerading as an ordinary Joe. It was probably what triggered Scott into secretly referring to him as the Death Salesman. His new friend – no, that wasn't right, they weren't friends, though Scott would like them to be – his new colleague was far from an ordinary Joe.

'Yeah, it's absolutely beautiful out here, isn't it?' Scott said. 'You'd never guess there's a hurricane on its way.'

The bartender delivered their drinks and this time she brought a complimentary bowl of nuts and pretzels. Perks seemed to gravitate to Joe Black, and Scott was happy to be along for the ride.

'Are you set up if it hits?'

'Absolutely.'

'Have extra room if I need some space for a couple of days?'

'Oh sure,' Scott told him and he sipped the Scotch, trying not to wince as it burned a path down his throat. 'One of the first things I did when I bought the place was replace the walk-in. This new one has plenty of space, extra shelves. It's top-of-the-line.'

In fact, he hadn't given a second thought to the hurricane. There had already been three this summer and none had ventured this far north into the Gulf. Scott had grown up in Michigan. Had no clue about hurricanes. Pensacola was Trish's hometown. In the two years he'd lived here he hadn't had to deal with the threat. When he bought the funeral home, he assumed it was set up for such things. He did know that there was an emergency generator, and if and when the time came he'd figure out how it worked or hire someone to do it for him.

Holmes and Meyers Funeral Home wasn't the first business Scott had run. Up in Michigan he had managed three funeral homes. Though this was the first one he'd owned, it wasn't any different. He was good at business, knew how to turn a profit, cut costs, and try innovative approaches to solving problems. He did what it took, like keeping the name even though no descendants of Holmes or Meyers worked at the place anymore. You couldn't put a dollar amount on the value of reputation, especially in the funeral business. Yeah, he was still a little nervous now that he was responsible for the place as well as for the huge banknote in his name. But his success was why Joe Black had chosen him and his funeral home in the first place.

'You're sticking around through the week?' Scott asked.

'I've got another conference in Destin on Monday. That's if they don't cancel because of the weather. I could use some storage space.'

'Oh sure. Bring whatever you have with you tomorrow. I'm sure I can make room. We're still on for tomorrow, right?'

'Absolutely.' He swirled the Scotch in his glass and turned to face Scott, giving him his attention. 'So, this is exciting. Your first indie.'

'Indie?'

'Indigent donor.'

'Oh, yeah.' Scott laughed, trying to hide his embarrassment. He needed to figure out the lingo or he'd never be cool. 'Who knew it would be so easy.'

'Already delivered?'

'And waiting.'

'Good.'

But now Joe's eyes were tracking someone or something just over Scott's shoulder. He glanced in the direction and sighed before he could catch himself.

'What?' Joe said. 'You know her?'

The object of Joe's distraction was the only woman at a table with four men. She seemed to be the center of attention, making them laugh.

'My sister-in-law.'

'Really?'

'Forget about her, though. I don't think she plays for our team.'

Joe looked at him and raised an eyebrow

49

but before Scott could explain, Joe's cell phone started ringing. He slipped it out of his shirt pocket, a razor-thin rectangle of silver and red that glowed pink when he opened it.

'This is Joe Black.'

Silence as Joe listened and ran an index finger over the rim of his glass. Scott caught himself watching out of the corner of his eye but he didn't want to look like he was eaves-dropping. He turned his barstool around, swinging it in the direction of Liz's table. She'd never notice him anyway. No one ever did. Besides, her table was at the restaurant next door.

Another glance and Scott saw that his father-in-law was one of the four men.

Now he almost wished they did see him, drinking expensive Scotch with a classy buddy. It would certainly give both of them a new image of him. And he wouldn't mind having an excuse for introducing Joe. Maybe even having them report back to Trish about his business dealings loosening him up. Isn't that what Trish was always telling him? That he needed to get out more? Instead he kept his back to Liz and his father-in-law. He pretended to be admiring the view.

'That's pretty short notice,' Joe said into the phone. 'No, I can do it. I'm just con-cerned how expensive it'll be for you.'

Scott wiped off a smile before Joe could catch it. What a salesman. He was telling some customer that he was going to charge him a ton of money and made it sound like he was only concerned about the client.

'Let me see what I can do and I'll get back to you tomorrow.'

No 'goodbye.' No 'thanks' or 'talk to you later.' Just a click and a flip.

'Always working,' Scott said.

'You know it,' Joe Black said. 'How about another one of these?'

He held up the glass and drained it in one gulp, not at all how Scott thought this expensive stuff should be drunk. But even as Joe called over the bartender, Scott could see him glance back over Scott's shoulder.

SEVEN

NAVAL AIR STATION
PENSACOLA, FLORIDA

Benjamin Platt insisted on seeing some of the worst cases. Yes, he was exhausted. Still a bit jet-lagged from the Afghanistan flight followed too soon by the one from D.C. to Florida, but he knew that if Captain Ganz took him to his hotel he wouldn't sleep. He'd be thinking about all these plastic tents with wounded soldiers waiting to find out what they'd been exposed to.

After examining just five soldiers, he grew more confused. Their injuries were all different. Their surgeries were different as well, but all were to repair limbs that had been severed, crushed, or otherwise damaged. Some were now amputees waiting to heal and be fitted with prosthetics. Many of the injuries – though it was always disheartening to see a soldier lose an arm or leg – were not necessarily life-threatening.

'Could it be something here at the hospital?' Platt asked Captain Ganz as they escaped to a lounge where they could be free of their masks and goggles and gloves.

'We haven't done anything differently. Nothing I can find that would suddenly be a problem.'

'You're thinking it might be something they were exposed to in Afghanistan? That perhaps they brought back with them?'

'Is that possible? Could a strain lie dormant?'

'And what? Come alive when you cut into them?'

Ganz wouldn't meet Platt's eyes, and Platt knew that must be exactly what the captain was most afraid of.

'There's nothing like that. Not that I'm aware of,' Platt told him.

'But it's not entirely impossible?'

Platt didn't have an answer. Two things his

years at USAMRIID had taught him were to never say never and that anything was possible.

'How many cases do you have isolated here?'

Ganz didn't have to stop to calculate. He knew off the top of his head. 'Seventy-six.'

'And for how long?'

'We started isolating eight days ago. But some of these soldiers had their surgical procedures up to eighteen days ago.'

'All of them were operated on here?'

'Yes, though some had temporary procedures done at Bagram before being flown here.'

'Any similarities there?'

'None that we've been able to isolate. Those who remain at Bagram haven't come down with the same symptoms. In fact, they haven't lost anyone in the same manner. You'd think that's where the problem should be.' Ganz attempted a laugh, but there was no humor, just frustration.

'You still have blood samples from the soldiers you lost. I'd like to take look at them.'

'Our lab has already examined them extensively–' But Ganz stopped and shook his head like a sleepwalker suddenly waking himself. He waved his hand as if to erase what he had said. 'Of course. I'll have someone set them up for you. What will you be looking for?'

Platt shrugged. 'Sometimes when we're focused on specifics, maybe particular pathogens like MRSA, we can miss other things that might not be so obvious.' He rubbed at his eyes, suddenly feeling the exhaustion again. *Methicillin resistant Staphylococcus aureus,* which surpassed HIV as the most deadly pathogen in the United States, was resistant to most antibiotics. It had become all too prevalent after surgical procedures, so it was one of the first things to look for when an infection resulted. 'I'll start by looking to see if there's any cell degradation.'

'You could probably use some sleep first. A few hours could help. I did pull you down here before you had a chance to catch your breath.'

'I'll be fine. Maybe some good strong coffee.'

The door to the lounge opened and a doctor in blue scrubs leaned inside, eyes urgent, not taking the time to enter.

'Captain, we're losing another one.'

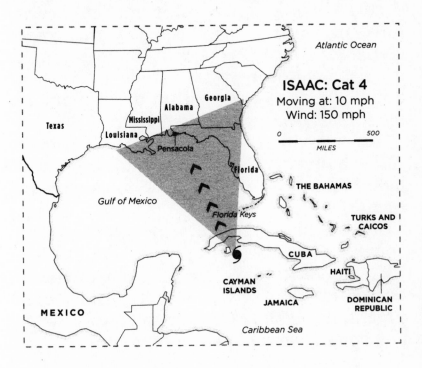

EIGHT

HARTSFIELD-JACKSON INTERNATIONAL AIRPORT ATLANTA, GEORGIA

Maggie's 6:00 am flight put her in Atlanta just before eight. Under two hours and it was still enough to rattle her composure. She hated flying – not the crowds, not the inconvenience, not even a fear of heights, but rather being trapped at thirty-eight thousand feet without any control. Even the upgrade to first class that Wurth managed to snag for her had done little to help.

He was waiting in baggage claim. For a small man he could deliver a body-crushing hug.

'Easy,' Maggie told him. 'What will people think?'

'Oh, it's okay here in Atlanta,' Wurth countered. 'But don't touch me once we leave the city and head into the South. You may even have to sit in the backseat so I can pretend I'm driving you.'

She rolled her eyes. She knew he was joking, but at the same time she knew there were still pockets in the South where a black man and a white woman in a vehicle together might draw some looks. But it couldn't be anything close to what they had already been through.

Maggie and Wurth had shared a terror-filled weekend last November. On the Friday following Thanksgiving, three young college students carrying backpacks loaded with explosives had blown up a section of Mall of America. Maggie and Wurth were dispatched to sort through the rubble and had tried to stop a second attack. In the end they had bonded against an unexpected and powerful enemy. It had been the beginning of Maggie's tumultuous relationship with her new boss, Assistant Director Raymond Kunze, and Charlie Wurth ended up becoming her ally, stepping in to defend her when Kunze would not.

'That's it?' Wurth said when she showed him her small Pullman. Dragging it behind her, she started leading him to the claims office to retrieve her firearm. 'O'Dell, for most women I know, that teeny thing would be their handbag.'

'Guess I'm not most women.'

'You're what we men call low maintenance. I've heard stories about low-maintenance women but I've never known one until now.'

With her gun safely holstered, Maggie followed Wurth outside to a black Escalade parked at the curb. An airport security officer had been watching over it and now opened the back while Wurth took Maggie's Pullman and lifted it in.

'Thanks, man.' Wurth reached up to pat the officer on his shoulder. He was at least a head taller than Wurth.

'You be safe,' the officer said as he opened the passenger door for Maggie.

Inside, the vehicle was spotless except for a pile of CD covers scattered in the console between them.

'I didn't realize rental places had these luxury SUVs anymore.'

'Oh, they probably don't.' Wurth turned the engine and blasted the AC. 'This one's not a rental. It's mine.'

'You're driving your personal vehicle down into a hurricane?'

'It's not about that.' He smiled and shook his head. 'We goin' down South, *cherie*. Into the middle of hurricane frenzy. A scrawny black man with a beautiful white woman – I'm packing all my necessary documents: registration, license, and proof of insurance, along with my badge.'

She laughed but Wurth wasn't laughing.

'You're serious.'

'As a heart attack.' He punched a couple of buttons on the dashboard and the sound of soft jazz filled the interior. 'We've got about five hours of interstate. How 'bout we hit Mickey D's drive-through for a couple of sausage biscuits?'

'In an Escalade with soft jazz? Sounds perfect.'

'Low, low maintenance,' he said. 'I'm liking this.'

She let him maneuver his way out of Hartfield-Jackson before she started prodding him.

'Have you learned anything since last night?'

'They have already unwrapped everything.' He glanced at her over his sunglasses. 'Sorry. I should have thought of it sooner. I'm not accustomed to dealing in body parts.'

'Don't worry about it. I'm sure they followed protocol.'

Maggie remembered what Tully had said about her becoming an expert. It wasn't the kind of thing she wished to add to her résumé.

'Turns out there were five packages: one male torso, one foot, and three hands.'

'Left or right?'

'Excuse me?'

'The hands and the foot. Were they left or right?'

This time he flashed an embarrassed grin. 'Again, sorry O'Dell. I didn't think to ask.' He shook his head. 'I thought my job had some interesting variables, but you got me beat.'

60

'Three hands? It's more than one victim.'

'So did we stumble on his trophies or his disposables?'

Maggie shrugged and leaned back in the leather captain seat. The car's AC was noiseless, chilling the interior as smoothly as the jazz filled it.

'A cooler this size could act as sort of a floating coffin, taking it farther out to sea. If the lid isn't locked, predators would take care of the remains, get rid of all the evidence. But the plastic wrapping suggests this guy didn't intend for the cooler to get away from him. I should be able to tell more once I see everything firsthand. Will I be able to visit the crime scene?'

'I was told that wouldn't be a problem.'

'And the cooler?'

'Waiting for you. The packages, however, are already with the ME. He'll take a look at them tomorrow morning. And yes, he's expecting your presence. You won't find much resistance. If anything, you might find a lack of interest. With this hurricane coming, the local law enforcement has more important things to worry about.'

'A storm is more important than a killer on the loose?'

Wurth glanced over at her as he turned into the parking lot of a McDonald's. 'You've never been in a hurricane before, huh?'

'That obvious?'

61

'Your killers carve up, what? Six bodies? A dozen over several months? Maybe several years? Isaac has already killed sixty-seven in forty-eight hours. This time, O'Dell, I think my killer trumps your killer.'

NINE

PENSACOLA, FLORIDA

Liz Bailey fumbled around the kitchen trying to fix breakfast, silently vowing that she would take time to buy the things she couldn't find. She hadn't lived in her father's house since high school. Her sister had lived here until she married Scott. That was two years ago – just enough time for her father to arrange things so that only he could find them.

She'd moved back in temporarily only because the housing she was promised with her transfer wouldn't be available for two months. Now searching for the toaster she wondered if she'd last that long.

She turned up the radio for the local weather report.

'Hurricane Isaac is expected to slam into the western side of Cuba today. Last night it bulldozed over Grand Cayman, flooding homes,

ripping off roofs, and toppling trees. More than half the homes on Grand Cayman are said to be damaged. And yet, Isaac hasn't lost any of its steam. It's now a cat 4 and traveling about ten miles an hour with sustained winds of 150 miles an hour. And guess what, folks, it's still expected to take that slight turn to the north/northeast, which means, you guessed it, we're smack-dab in the middle of its path. Landfall may be sometime Wednesday. Time to start boarding up, stocking up, and moving out, folks.'

'They're always wrong,' her dad said as he shuffled in, still in his pajamas though he had been up for an hour reading the newspaper and drinking coffee.

Finally, the toaster! Liz found it in the bottom cabinet under the sink. Of course, the last place she'd think to look. She pulled it out without any comment. Trish would have commented, scolded, and instructed where the toaster should be stored.

'Not this time, Dad. The CG and the NHC has the Florida Panhandle in the crosshairs.'

'Well, that's not where the media says it's gonna hit. They're all in New Orleans again, ready and waiting. This morning's *Journal* has the projected path drawn from Galveston to Tampa, and they all act like New Orleans is the only place they give a damn about.'

'You should get gas today. And batteries

63

and bottled water. Won't Trish and Scott need to come stay with you? They can't stay on the bay.'

'I've got a whole container of batteries and plenty of bottled water in the garage. Enough food in the refrigerators to feed us for a week.'

'You'll need a generator just to keep your three refrigerators running.'

'I've got three generators.'

'Then you better get gas today, Dad. Will you do that? Will you promise me you'll get the gas cans filled today?'

'Sure, sure.'

'You won't put it off?'

'I'll go out before lunch. But you're not gonna be here anyway. Where will they send you?'

'Probably Jacksonville. Someplace out of the path but close enough we can fly in immediately after. Remember, I told you. We came in right behind Katrina, so close I could see the swell of the backstorm. I imagine we'll try to do the same this time.'

'Those boys sure have taken a liking to you.' He filled his coffee cup, standing beside her as she waited for the toaster to spit out her bagel.

'Yeah, we're all a bunch of buddies.' She wanted to add that it was easy to be buddies after a few beers, but she'd never let her dad know that it was anything different.

'They have a small article in the *Journal* about that cooler you brought up yesterday.'

'Really?'

'Front page. Bottom right-hand corner. I set it aside for you.'

'Tell me what they said.' She slathered cream cheese on her toasted bagel and took a bite. Her dad read every inch of the daily *Pensacola News Journal* and could usually repeat almost verbatim the articles he took an interest in.

'Suspicious fishing cooler retrieved by the Coast Guard,' he told her, while tipping little splashes of cream into his coffee like he was rationing it. 'It didn't mention anything about the contents or even suggest foul play or that it had body parts inside.'

Liz almost choked on her bagel.

'Why do you think there were body parts?'

'It's okay. I won't say anything to anybody. The little guy, the one who had all the hot dogs and couldn't hold his liquor – Tommy? He let it slip about the foot. He said there was other stuff, too, so I'm just assuming there might be the rest of a body.'

So much for all their training. Liz knew Wilson and Ellis were green, but this was ridiculous. The entire aircrew could get suspended for something like this.

'You know there was an article in last week's *Journal*. Someplace up near Washington, D.C. A possible serial killer. One of

65

those sick bastards who kept pieces of his victim. Maybe this is related.'

'Dad, I can't talk about it. You know I can't discuss this.'

'I'm just talking about the news.'

He struggled with a bagel for himself, trying to cut it in half with a bread knife. Liz gently took it from him, twisted it apart, and dropped both halves in the toaster.

'Okay, so tell me what you read about the serial killer.'

TEN

NORTH SEVENTEENTH AVENUE UNDERPASS PENSACOLA, FLORIDA

Billy Redding hit the jackpot. His battered shopping cart rattled with stacked aluminum cans. He crushed as many as he could until his hands were sore. The curse of small hands. In fact, Billy had convinced himself years ago that it had always been his worthless little hands that had prevented him from being successful in life. But maybe his luck was turning. Now with most of the cans crushed and almost flat, he could fit another two dozen into the cart.

Saturday nights always left a jackpot in the Wayside Park trash barrels. The trick, Billy had discovered, was to get here early enough on Sunday to beat the city's cleanup crew. Cashing in this pile would take care of him for a week.

He headed back to the underpass to hide his stash. The short distance exhausted him. He was out of breath when he heard a car coming from behind him. Billy pushed back onto the curb to get out of the way. The car slowed. Billy kept moving uphill, panting in the morning humidity. His T-shirt stuck to his back like a second skin. He hated that and wore a long-sleeve button-down shirt over it, thinking it would act as a layer of insulation or at least soak up the extra moisture. He didn't mind being hot. He hated being wet. Bugs would get tangled in his beard whenever it got wet. That's why he learned to stick close to the underpass. It provided shelter from the rain.

'Hey, Billy,' someone called out to him.

He wanted to pretend he didn't hear them. He needed to keep going. But sometimes people stopped and gave him a couple of bucks. He glanced over his shoulder.

A police cruiser. Damn!

He stopped immediately. Secured the shopping cart with a rock under one of the back wheels. A big rock he carried strictly for that purpose.

As he got closer to the car Billy recognized the orange-haired cop. Sometimes they told him their names but he never remembered. He was always polite. As long as he was polite, they were polite back. So Billy just kept his head down and answered their questions, said 'yes' a lot and called them 'sir.' Once he even called a female cop 'sir.' He was so embarrassed that he couldn't stutter out an apology. She ended up giving him five bucks and said not to worry about it.

'There's a hurricane coming this way, Billy,' the cop told him through the rolled-down window of the cruiser.

'Yes, sir.'

'When the time comes I'll send someone here to pick you up. You're going to need to go to a hurricane shelter. Do you understand, Billy? You won't be able to stay out here.'

'Yes, sir. Will I be able to bring my shopping cart?'

'They'll have food and everything else you'll need at the shelter.'

Billy kept his head down and kicked at the curb. 'It's hard to find these.'

The cop was quiet and out of the corner of his eyes Billy could see him shaking his head.

'Sure, Billy. We'll figure something out. I'll tell them you can bring your cart.'

Billy bagged some of the cans and put them in his safe spot, a deserted grassy hide-away several yards from the underpass. If he hurried back to the park, he might be able to grab more cans before the cleanup crew arrived. He couldn't go to the recycling kiosk until tomorrow. It'd take a whole day.

His cart rattled even more now with only half the crushed cans to jump around. Billy liked the jingle-jangle. It reminded him of the sound of loose change in his daddy's trouser pocket. 'Ice-cream money,' he'd call it and the two of them would laugh at their secret code so Billy's mama wouldn't know they were really going out to buy and share a cheap bottle of vodka.

Billy had just gotten to the park when he heard another vehicle pull in behind him. He moved out of the way but the van stopped alongside him.

'Hey,' a man called out.

Billy kept going, glancing back at the van. The man wore dark sunglasses and rested his arm out the window. Billy noticed a patch on the shoulder. A uniform. Like a cop. Had they sent someone to get him already? He stopped and looked up into the clear-blue sky then turned toward the water of the bay. The waves churned over the ledge but it didn't look like a hurricane was coming.

'You need to come with me,' the man said to him. 'I know it looks like a nice day, but there's a hurricane on the way.'

'Yes, sir. I know that.' Billy stayed on the curb. 'They told me I could bring my shopping cart.'

The man stared at him. Billy decided he wouldn't go if they didn't let him take the shopping cart.

'Sure, I've got room.' The man climbed out of the van and slid open the side door, ready to help Billy. 'You probably should climb in beside it and keep it from tipping.'

As Billy started to crawl inside, stepping over all the bags of ice, he tried to remember if any of the other cops wore khaki shorts and really nice deck shoes. That was his last thought as the rock cracked the back of his skull.

ELEVEN

NAVAL AIR STATION PENSACOLA, FLORIDA

Benjamin Platt cut himself again as the tiny bathroom fixtures shook and clattered from the vibration. Overhead, the steady buzz of airplanes and helicopters taking off continued. There would be no break anytime soon, and Platt's attempt at shaving was leaving him with enough nicks and scars that he considered growing a beard.

The latest weather reports had the eye of Hurricane Isaac heading straight for the Florida Panhandle, even though the storm hadn't entered the Gulf of Mexico yet. The base wasn't taking any chances. The naval flight school had called in pilots, flight instructors, and even students to fly aircraft to safer ground. And this morning the admiral was adamant about moving the quarantined soldiers to safer ground as well.

Platt had escaped late last night to get a couple hours' rest, though sleep didn't come easily. He couldn't get the image of the young soldier out of his mind. By the time Platt found Captain Ganz, the admiral had already called. Platt only witnessed the aftermath. Ganz had been unnerved about losing yet another patient, but the admiral's insistence on an evacuation of the makeshift isolation ward left the captain angry and frustrated. He was depending on Platt to find some answers and find them quickly.

Now as Platt headed over to the lab to participate in the autopsy, he felt a new weight on his shoulders. He hadn't even had a chance to look at the blood samples. Ganz was in a hurry, not just to come up with answers before another soldier collapsed but also to beat the storm. Platt wanted to tell him to slow down. He wanted to tell him that sometimes these things took weeks, months to figure out. But he knew that was exactly why Ganz had requested his presence. The captain was placing all his bets on Platt discovering some hidden virus, some new deadly strain of bacteria. He expected a miracle. And from what Platt had seen in the short amount of time since his arrival, he knew – barring a miracle – there would be no immediate answers.

He kept thinking about the young soldier who died last night. They said he had vomited green liquid just before falling into a coma. By the time Platt saw him, he looked remarkably peaceful. A single groan escaped his lips while his body struggled to get enough oxygen. There had been no swelling around his incision. No fever, though it was apparent from the wet bedsheets that he had perspired immensely in the preceding hours. The pupils of his eyes were not dilated nor had the blood vessels burst. Only in the last hour had his heart rate slowed and his blood pressure plummeted. He never regained consciousness. Whatever had infected these young soldiers was deceitful, clever, and lethal.

TWELVE

MONTGOMERY, ALABAMA

Gasoline exploded over the top of the can and splattered on Maggie's shoes before she snapped the pump off.

'Damn it, Wurth. Tell me again why the deputy director of Homeland Security is filling gas cans to haul in his SUV. Aren't you supposed to be arranging for trucks and caravans of trucks to deliver things to the hurricane victims?'

'What victims? This is my personal stash. Just put that last can next to the stack of bottled water.'

Maggie slipped off her shoes and threw them in the back with the supplies. The asphalt burned her feet before she got back to the passenger side of the SUV. She opened her window despite the scorching heat. The fumes were already giving her a headache, and by her own calculations they had another three hours on the road.

Wurth slid into the driver's seat and handed her an ice-cold can of Diet Pepsi, his idea of a peace offering. She accepted.

'You'll be thanking me that I got a whole

six-pack on ice back there for you. By the time we get down to Pensacola most of the shelves will be picked clean. Gas stations will either have long lines or be sold out. And there is absolutely nothing worse than being stuck in a hurricane area just because you can't get enough gasoline to drive away.'

'I thought you weren't supposed to drive away. I thought you were supposed to be the cavalry.'

Charlie Wurth laughed and shook his head. 'Where do you come up with these ideas, O'Dell?'

'You never did tell me why you're being dispatched to the Florida Panhandle when your home is New Orleans. Isn't New Orleans in this storm's path, too?'

'New Orleans is where all the media is.' He pulled the SUV back into interstate traffic.

When Maggie realized that was the end of his explanation, she prodded. 'Yes, so that's where all the media is and...?'

'You know how this works better than I do. You've been a part of this federal bureaucracy longer than me. Media's all set up in the Big Easy then that's where the director is. Not the deputy director.'

Of course. She couldn't believe she hadn't guessed.

'Which reminds me' – Wurth threw her a glance – 'maybe now's a good time for you to tell me how you managed to get yourself smack-dab in the line of fire yesterday.'

'Is that what you heard?'

'That's what I was told.'

She shouldn't have been surprised that Kunze would characterize the incident as her fault.

'What exactly did my boss tell you?'

'I won't tell you his exact words because I don't use that kind of language in front of a lady, but I believe the gist of what he said was that you screwed up. Didn't see it coming.'

'I didn't see it coming?'

Maggie couldn't believe it. How dare Kunze blame her for a killer's unpredictable behavior. And to suggest it publicly to someone outside the bureau. What would be next? Saying that it was her negligence that made him fire his own gun three times into the killer? The first shot had been enough to stop him. Maggie wondered if the head shot that splattered her with the killer's brains had simply been overkill to do just that – splatter her.

'Did he even tell you what happened?'

'Maybe you should tell me what happened.'

'Or my version. Isn't that what you're really saying?'

'Hey, I'm on your side, O'Dell.' He held his hands up in surrender then dropped them back to the steering wheel. 'If I believed anything Kunze said, you wouldn't be on this road trip with me.'

'You're right. I'm sorry.'

'You know what, it doesn't even matter what happened. You found the son of a bitch, right? And now he's out of commission. From what I read in last week's newspapers there were a few body parts involved in that case, too.'

She waited for him to make the same inference Tully had – that somehow she'd become an expert in murders that included body parts. Wurth glanced at her.

'As far as I'm concerned,' he said, 'you did us all a favor.'

Maggie settled into the oversize captain seat, tucking a bare foot underneath her, looking out the window, but her mind returned to yesterday's bizarre shooting. They had tracked down and found ... no, that wasn't right. *She* had tracked down and found the killer's torture chamber – a deserted warehouse near the Potomac.

For Maggie it brought back memories of another killer she had caught many years ago. Sometimes she worried that all the killers she had come in contact with were morphing together. That Assistant Director Kunze had shot and killed this one didn't even bother her. She agreed with Wurth. It meant another monster wouldn't be hurting another innocent victim. That she didn't predict he would be there, who cared?

She had dug deep enough into his psyche to figure out where he hid, where he kept his dirty little secret life. Shouldn't that have been enough? Why had Kunze expected her to read his mind? Didn't Kunze realize that to dig deeper meant inching her way too close to the edge? Or maybe that was exactly what Kunze wanted. To shove her and see if she'd fall.

THIRTEEN

PENSACOLA BEACH

Liz Bailey downed her second Red Bull. She checked and rechecked the flight equipment then packed it back where it belonged. She had already gone over medical equipment piece by piece, even though they hadn't used anything yesterday. She was bored, only it was worse, waiting and knowing, the calm before the storm. Staying alert while staying put and waiting.

In their briefing this morning they were told to prepare to be on emergency standby for the rest of the week. She could see the waves from her post, churning and bucking against the seawall. Surfers were out before she arrived. She knew they'd be here until authorities made them leave and closed the beach. And they'd grumble about leaving, their eyes glazed over with adrenaline. You just didn't get waves like the ones that came right before a hurricane.

Several of the hotels had started encouraging guests to check out, but the beach was still packed with tourists. Other than the waves there was no indication of a storm, the sky still cloudless and blue, the sun baking the white sand. The last August days before vacations ended for another year. Why would anyone believe they needed to leave this paradise and go home early?

The rest of Liz's aircrew were down the beach a mile at the heliport, crawling over their helicopter, doing their own pre-flight assessments, checks, and rechecks. She usually enjoyed the alone time. Today it added to her restlessness. They had been instructed to sit tight and wait. All they were told was that the deputy director of Homeland Security and an FBI investigator were on their way. It sounded like they would be taking over the case. Liz thought it a waste of time for them to be grilled all over again. What new questions could they ask? What more information could their aircrew provide?

She remembered what her dad had said

about body parts and felt a bit sick to her stomach. How stupid could Tommy Ellis be? But then how stupid had all four of them been? Sure, Wilson prodded them to open the cooler, but Kesnick should never have gone any further once they realized what they had found. It was Kesnick who pulled out each piece. Except the large one, the one they agreed looked like a torso. The plastic had been wrapped tight but it yielded enough that they could see the parts had been sliced clean. No rips or tears. Whoever had done this knew exactly where to cut and had the tools to do an efficient job.

Now Liz wondered if Kesnick confessed to the authorities yesterday how much he had handled the wrapped pieces. Liz certainly hadn't said a word. She didn't lie. But for all the questions, no one thought about asking, 'Did you handle the contents? Do you know what you found?'

Instead, the authorities were more concerned with where the cooler had been discovered and whether or not they had talked to anyone on the ground about it. Anyone outside their aircrew. Even later, when the four of them went out for drinks and hot dogs, they stayed away from the topic. Or at least, Liz thought they had. When was it that Tommy Ellis had slipped and told her dad? Had Ellis told anyone else?

She suspected that the deputy director of Homeland Security and the FBI agent would ask more pointed questions. Ones that couldn't be evaded as easily. Would they dare suspend them all with a hurricane coming?

Liz saw a sleek, black SUV loop around the parking lot, an Escalade with Louisiana license plates. It didn't park, though there were plenty of empty spaces in front of the building. Instead, it headed back onto Via De Luna Drive. She watched until it turned off into the Hilton Hotel.

They were here.

Her nerves tensed, and she wished she hadn't had that second Red Bull.

FOURTEEN

Scott Larsen hadn't taken time to change out of his suit from Sunday-morning service at First United Christ. Trish was used to him dropping her off at home before he headed over to the funeral home, but this morning she had been on edge about the hurricane.

'We need to start thinking about what we're going to do,' she nagged at him all the way home. 'We probably need some plywood to board up the patio doors.'

'The thing hasn't even gotten into the Gulf

yet,' Scott had countered.

He was impatient with all this worry over something that might not even come their way. Besides, he hated leaving Joe Black the run of his embalming room. The guy insisted Scott give him a key and security code so he could start work. Other than accepting delivery and providing temporary cold storage of a few specimens for Black to pick up en route to one of his doctors' conferences, *this* was their first real business dealing.

After months of listening to Joe Black talk – actually there was more insinuation than talk – about the impressive network, the major connections to doctors and medical equipment companies, and all the 'big money' there was waiting to be made, Scott had jumped at the chance when Black finally invited him to be a major player. And Scott had already been paid handsomely for the storage fees. It was Joe who told him how to contract with the county to handle indigents. That little tip would bring in five hundred dollars a shot, just for accepting and processing the bodies. Plus, Joe Black was going to pay him another five hundred each. Scott didn't have to lift a finger.

It was a win-win situation. He couldn't believe his good fortune. And it came at just the right time. Trish had long ago overspent their budget on the house they were building. He hadn't told her that he decided to forgo buying hurricane insurance for it. How was he supposed to afford it when they were still paying renter's insurance on their condo plus the insurance on the funeral home? Now it was too late. He couldn't buy insurance after the first of June, when hurricane season started. This one sure as hell better take a turn and stay far away. Then he reminded himself that it wasn't even in the Gulf.

Some days he truly felt like a transplant down here in Florida. Just last week someone at one of his memorial services called him 'a Yankee' and jokingly told him, 'But maybe you won't become a "damn Yankee."'

'What's a damn Yankee?' Scott wanted to know.

'One that stays.'

Days like this, Scott wondered why he hadn't insisted they live in Michigan. He'd been lured by those emerald-green waters and sandy beaches. And Trish in a bikini, though she hardly ever wore one now that they were married, even though they lived right on the bay.

Scott drove around the one-story funeral home that looked remarkably like an oversize ranch house. Every time he pulled into the parking lot he felt a swell of pride. It was all his ... his and the bank's: three viewing rooms, chapel, visitors' lounge, and corner office. The embalming room and storage facility were in a separate building that connected to the back of the funeral home via an air-conditioned walkway.

He'd added the twenty-five-foot walkway. It was crazy going even that short distance in a suit and tie and getting sweaty from the humidity or drenched from a downpour. He insisted on presenting a clean, crisply pressed appearance. Likewise, his entire place was kept meticulously.

The public areas – the viewing rooms and visitors' lounge – were vacuumed daily, stocked with fresh flowers, furniture aligned at straight angles with ample room for foot traffic as well as coffin traffic. Even the back area that included the embalming room and walk-in refrigerator was spotless. The stainless-steel tables and shelves gleamed. The white linoleum floors and porcelain basins always had a glossy finish. The state inspectors constantly praised Scott and told him they wished all the places they had to inspect looked this good.

Now as he pulled up to the back door his eyes darted around, looking for a vehicle. Joe Black had been driving something different every time they'd met. Scott figured he must use various leased cars or perhaps rentals. Last night Joe had walked up the beach so Scott hadn't even seen what he was driving. But there wasn't a vehicle anywhere in sight. Could he have finished already? Or maybe he hadn't started yet.

Scott disarmed the alarm system and had his key in the door when he heard something rattling against the back of the building. He stopped and leaned around the corner. A rusted old shopping cart had been wedged between the trunk of a magnolia tree and his Dumpster.

Damn! He hated people snooping around his property, leaving trash. It cost money to empty that frickin' Dumpster.

He was shaking his head, still cursing under his breath, when he went inside. He immediately reset the alarm.

Scott understood that there were specific reasons why he had become a mortician. He didn't really like working with people. Sure, he had to advise and guide the bereaved, but it was easier to work with people when they were at their most vulnerable. They automatically looked to him as the expert. There was a built-in respect that came with the job title.

He actually didn't mind working with dead people. Trish insisted that much of what he did was creepy and gross: the make-up, hairstyling, and clothes. Sometimes he had to paint the skin or sew up leaking orifices. And there were the plastic lenses he inserted beneath the eyelids to keep the eyes from popping open in the middle of a memorial.

Even the blood didn't bother him. You drained it out and replaced it with embalming fluid. Oh sure, you couldn't avoid blood leaking out sometimes, but it never sprayed or splattered like it did from a live, pumping heart. And yet, despite all the awkward and messy jobs Scott had done, nothing had prepared him for what he saw.

He backed up and stayed in the doorway, his hand pressed against the wall, needing it to steady himself.

Pink liquid pooled on the white linoleum floor and filled the troughs alongside the stainless-steel tables. A cardboard box blocked his entry, the type Scott used for bodies transported to the crematory, only this one held wadded-up bundles of clothes. On one of the tables lay a torso – the head, arms, and legs gone. On the other lay a corpse. It looked peaceful until Scott realized its knees and feet were cut off and lying in between its legs.

Joe Black stood at the counter. When he turned around, Scott saw the front of his lab gown, his latex gloves, and his shoe covers, all soaked with blood.

'Oh hey, Scott, you're just in time. I could use some help.'

FIFTEEN

Maggie stared at the helicopter and the orange flight suit being handed to her. Obviously she hadn't given it enough thought when she asked to see the crime scene. It was the Coast Guard, for God's sake. Didn't they use boats?

A helicopter. She felt her knees go a bit weak. She could barely handle being trapped on a commercial airliner. How the hell was she supposed to do a helicopter?

'Wouldn't it be easier to take a look from a boat?' she asked, still not accepting the flight suit that the young woman offered.

She hoped the question didn't sound ridiculous. Already she felt a bit sick to her stomach just from the thought of climbing into the helicopter. She pushed her sunglasses up and crossed her arms, pretending it was no big deal how they proceeded. She didn't want the aircrew to interpret her hesitancy as fear. The slip, the tell would not be a great start to the investigation, and it would certainly hamper her credibility, let alone her authority. A refusal or even hesitancy would be a mistake, especially with this macho group. All of them were young (with the exception of Pete Kesnick), lean, and muscular, even the woman, the rescue swimmer named Elizabeth Bailey.

Earlier Maggie had watched Bailey don her wet suit instead of a flight suit, slipping the formfitting one-piece over the plain white shorts and white CG tank top that showed off her tanned, long legs and broad shoulders but failed to hide her femininity – full breasts and small waist. She wore her sun-bleached hair short, easy to slip under the wet suit's hood which she kept at the back of her neck, ready instead for the flight helmet she held under her arm.

'We're the crew that found the cooler,' the pilot, Lieutenant Commander Wilson, told Maggie. 'We're an aircrew.' He was saying it slowly as though explaining it to a child and Maggie realized she had no choice. 'Is there a problem?'

During their introductions she had detected an air of annoyance from Wilson. Forever the profiler she had already decided it wasn't due to the inconvenience but rather that he believed what Maggie was asking was somehow beneath his pay grade. At first she thought his reaction might be a knee-jerk prejudice against Wurth as a black authority figure or herself as a woman. Wurth had left after the introductions to begin his own pre-hurricane duties. And since Wilson's attitude hadn't left with Wurth, Maggie realized she might be the one Wilson had a problem with. It was silly to give his prejudices any credence.

'No problem,' Maggie answered. 'Just hate to take you away from more important things.'

Wilson nodded, satisfied. The other two men, Kesnick and Ellis, simply returned to their preparations. But Bailey caught Maggie's eyes as she offered the flight suit again. And in that brief exchange, Maggie realized that Bailey had recognized her fear. Would the woman give her away? Put Maggie in her place?

Bailey handed Maggie the suit, holding on to it a count longer than necessary. With her back turned to the men she let Maggie see that she was slipping something into the flight suit's pocket.

'It's gonna be choppy out there today,' Bailey told her. 'Be sure to buckle in tight.'

Then she left to pack the rest of her own gear, including a small bag with basic medical supplies. That's when Maggie remembered that rescue swimmers were also certified EMTs.

Maggie slipped off her shoes and started putting on the flight suit. The aircrew no longer took any interest in her as they completed their preparations. She fingered the plastic inside the pocket, cupping it in the palm of her hand before bringing out two

88

pink-and-white capsules.

Dramamine? Benadryl? Neither worked for her.

It wasn't about motion sickness. It was about losing control. It was a thoughtful and gracious gesture, and on closer inspection Maggie noticed the capsules were not over-the-counter medication. Instead, the small print on the plastic package read: *Zingiber officinale.*

She looked up at Bailey but the young woman was climbing into the helicopter. Maggie's nausea started to churn as she watched the others putting on their helmets and gloves. Soon her heart would start to race, followed by the cold sweats.

What the hell, she thought. Maybe the capsules were something new they gave to rescued survivors. Or maybe it was some prank to make the FBI lady sicker than a dog. At this point, Maggie realized that she was willing to take her chances.

She tugged open the plastic, popped the capsules into her mouth, and dry-swallowed them. Then she pulled on her helmet and headed for the helicopter, trying to ignore the wobble in her knees.

SIXTEEN

Scott worried that he might throw up. He'd never seen body pieces. Not like this, carved and lined up, set out to rinse and wrap. His face must have registered his discomfort.

'How did you think it was done, buddy?' Joe Black asked, pushing his goggles up onto his tousled hair. 'Unfortunately, there's nothing dignified about disarticulating a body. It's a messy job.'

'I guess I just ... it's not what I expected.'

He couldn't move. Couldn't stop his eyes from darting around the room. He didn't want to step over the cardboard coffin stretched out in front of him. He didn't want to step into the room at all.

'You'll get used to it,' Joe assured him.

Joe picked up what looked like an ordinary carving knife. He glanced at Scott, caught him wincing, and put the knife back down.

'It's a bit weird at first.' There was no condescending tone, more instructive like a teacher to a student. 'You learn a lot by simply doing it. A bit of trial and error. Actually, it's not that different from carving a Thanksgiving turkey.' He smiled at Scott.

Joe turned back to the counter, picked up

one of the pieces. Scott couldn't tell what it was. He didn't want to look and yet he found himself mesmerized by Joe's hands pulling plastic wrap and folding it over and over with a slow, almost reverent touch.

'I try not to be wasteful,' Joe continued, keeping his back to Scott as he started wrapping the next piece in line. 'It's the least we can do when people are generous enough to donate their bodies. Right? Every week surgeons are learning some new, innovative technique. And they'd never be able to do that without me providing working models.'

Scott appreciated that Joe didn't draw attention to his reaction. Instead, Joe remained calm while Scott was acting like a total jerk. He knew exactly what he had signed up for and had read plenty about the subject. He had no illusions about what were in the previous packages that Joe Black had sent to him to store. Although he had to admit that it was certainly easier when he could accept the UPS or FedEx deliveries and cart the packages into his walk-in refrigerator or put them in one of his freezers.

All along he knew the packages contained body parts that were used for educational conferences and for research. Early on Joe had bragged about the surgical conferences that were his specialty. On paper and in his mind, Scott Larsen had justified the extra income as a noble service. So he needed to get over his squeamishness.

Like embalming and cremation, this, too, was just business.

'You really have a nice facility here,' Joe told him, glancing around as he started to work on the torso that was left on the other table. 'And don't worry. I'll clean everything up. Get it sparkling the way you had it.'

'Oh, I'm not worried about that.'

Scott hated to think Joe might believe he had a problem with any of this. In an attempt to restore their camaraderie Scott tried to take interest in what Joe was doing. 'So I guess you have orders for all these different ... parts?'

'More orders than I can supply.' He took out a jar of Vicks VapoRub, dipped a gob, and started smearing it on the torso. 'It's hard to keep up.'

'What's that you're doing?'

'A little trick of the trade. The torsos are popular with medical-device companies to showcase their new equipment, to teach a new technique. Sometimes the surgeons'll work on them for several hours and, well, I don't have to tell you. A couple of hours and you know how bad it'll start smelling.'

'Oh sure.'

'I rub Vicks VapoRub into the skin before I freeze it. Then when it defrosts it smells like menthol. Which is much better than what it ordinarily smells like.'

'Wow. That's really ... smart.'

'You morticians have plenty of your own tricks, right? You guys are like magicians when it comes to making corpses look good. Sometimes even better than what they looked like when they were alive.'

'Families have high expectations.'

Before Scott realized it, Joe had him talking about his own techniques. He even told Joe how he cheated sometimes and left off the socks and shoes because he hated dealing with feet. He couldn't even remember when he stepped over the cardboard coffin and came into the room. Soon he was gowned up, rinsing and wrapping, and telling more stories. Even made Joe laugh a couple of times. They cleaned up the room together and planned to meet for drinks later in the evening on the beach.

Scott had gotten so carried away, actually having a good time, that it wasn't until after Joe had left that he realized he'd never asked where he parked. Nor had he dared to ask him about the second body.

SEVENTEEN

Liz watched the FBI agent grip the leather restraints in her gloved fists. She was pretty good at feigning confidence, making it sound like this ride was no big deal, even asking questions about the fishing cooler in sound bites as though she was used to the abrupt shouting conversations of a heli-copter. Despite all that, she hadn't fooled Liz at all. For whatever reason, the woman had panicked back there on the beach the minute she realized she'd need to climb into the copter.

So far O'Dell appeared to be doing okay. But just as Wilson turned the helicopter around after hovering over the spot where they had found the cooler yesterday, a call came in. A boat had capsized. A recrea-tional-fishing cabin cruiser. At least one person was in the water. Initial radio contact reported injuries. Contact since had been lost.

'Sorry, Agent O'Dell,' Wilson shouted over his helmet mike. 'We won't have time to drop you off.'

That's when Liz first noticed O'Dell's white-knuckled grip. Now she wondered if the FBI agent would last. Liz couldn't ask whether she had taken the capsules she'd slipped to her. Though they were definitely not a miracle cure, she hoped O'Dell had trusted her. Otherwise she'd be feeling sick very soon. In the short time since they left the beach the winds had picked up over the Gulf. Away from shore, the seas were kicking high. And now, so was Liz's adrenaline.

They found the boat quickly. Liz kept her helmet on, staying connected to their ICS while they figured this one out.

The cabin cruiser had tilted but hadn't rolled yet. The waves were battering it and had already broken apart some of the cockpit and the rail. One person bobbed in the water, not more than a head in a life jacket with an arm hanging on to a torn piece of the cockpit that dangled, barely attached to the boat. A dog, what looked to Liz like a black Labrador, paced the deck, watching his owner while trying to keep his balance.

'Radio's completely out?' Kesnick asked.

'Doesn't matter. He can't reach it,' Ellis said.

'Looks like only one rescue,' Wilson said.

'We can't drop the basket in the water,' Kesnick told them. 'Current will pull them under the boat.'

'Then where the hell are you dropping it?' Wilson asked.

Liz glanced at O'Dell, who was watching

95

her prepare. Was O'Dell wondering why the men didn't ask what she thought?

Silently Liz was planning her own strategy. Stay away from that railing. Don't put any extra weight on the tip-side or it'll roll. The boat was moving with the current, and as soon as Wilson dropped into hover the rotor wash would set the boat rocking. Initial radio contact reported injuries. If they dropped the basket onto the tilted boat, Liz would have to find a way to roll him out of the water debris, back onto the boat, and into the rescue basket.

'Direct deployment's gonna be tricky,' Kesnick was saying. 'Don't push it or strain yourself. Let me do the dropping.'

Liz realized he was talking to her. She looked up at him.

'Let me do the heavy lifting, Bailey. We may need to quick strop him just to get him into the basket. Get it under his arms and let me hoist him while you guide him into the basket. Okay? I don't wanna lose you both under that damned boat. You got that?'

She nodded. Gave him a thumbs-up. Let out a long breath. She started to remove her helmet when she heard Wilson.

'We've got one rescue, Bailey. Unless you find someone else in the water, that basket is only coming up once. We're not sending it down again for that dog. You understand, Bailey? This isn't New Orleans after Katrina. That dog is not coming up. It'll have to wait for the cutter.'

She yanked off the helmet without a response. As Liz tucked her hair into her surf hood and strapped on her Seda helmet, she purposely avoided O'Dell's eyes.

She readjusted her harness and rechecked her restraints. Her adrenaline was pumping and she needed to calm it down a notch, just enough to let it work for her, not against her. They could talk all they wanted, analyze and discuss to the last detail, but once she was out on that cable it was Liz who'd be balancing on the edge of that tilted cruiser. It'd be up to Liz to maneuver the survivor before a lift could even be made. And it'd be Liz's ass if it didn't work.

She scooted into position at the door. Kesnick waited for her glance then held her eyes a beat longer than usual. 'Let me help you on this.' Maybe he had read her mind.

She nodded and he tapped her chest. She gave him a thumbs-up and crawled out. She slid down just a few feet to stop and wait for the hoist cable to tighten, but instead the wind caught it. The cable looped and bucked then jerked Liz like she was hanging on to the end of a whip. The rotor wash twisted her, pushing her in one direction then the other. Another jerk wrenched her spine. That's when she started to spin. It was like getting sucked up into a wind tunnel.

97

All Liz could see was a blur as she hung tight to the cable. She closed her eyes and dug her heels down around the cable, managing to keep her feet crossed at the ankles. She tucked her chin into her chest so the cable didn't wind around her neck. She made her body as rigid as possible.

She did everything she was taught to do. But the spin only accelerated.

EIGHTEEN

Maggie watched the rescue swimmer jump out of the helicopter one minute and within seconds she saw the flight mechanic, Kesnick, stumble and slide, diving headfirst toward the open door as if he were being sucked out behind Bailey.

Maggie reacted on instinct. She ripped at her restraints, her gloved fingers taking too long to break herself free. She grabbed for his safety belt that remained hooked into the deck of the cabin. She hadn't even seen the hoist cable snag Kesnick's helmet. Instead, she followed the safety belt's line, using its tautness to pull herself to her feet.

She heard Wilson and Ellis trying to figure out what the hell was going on. She couldn't see them and didn't take precious time to wait until she could. Instead, she gripped Kesnick's belt and pulled with all her weight. It was enough to jerk Kesnick out of his freefall stance. But the hoist cable that had caught his helmet still whipped his head back in the direction of the open door.

Kesnick let out a scream from the pain. For a brief, sick moment, Maggie worried it might have broken his neck. Her eyes followed the cable from its snag on his helmet to a hook on the top of the open door. She couldn't reach the hoist cable but she could reach his helmet. She clawed at it, trying to remember what clicked into what.

Wilson and Ellis were yelling at each other, at Kesnick, at Maggie. Then the helicopter shifted and rocked, slinging Kesnick backward, his head in her gut. His helmetless head. Thank God. She saw the cable snap and fling Kesnick's helmet out the door.

Maggie grabbed on to a leather strap attached to the wall just as the helicopter rocked again and her feet started to slide toward the door. Wilson grunted a string of curses before he rocked it back and held steady.

Amazingly Kesnick was already on his knees crawling back to his feet.

Ellis yelled, 'Are you okay, man?'

But without his helmet, Kesnick didn't hear and couldn't respond. He hurried back to the open doorway, clutching his safety belt still tethered by the line to the floor. He leaned out to look down for Bailey. Maggie had forgotten about the rescue swimmer. Was she still even there? Kesnick reached for the hoist cable, wrestling and jerking it until the loop that had knotted on the hook broke loose. Somehow he managed to tug it free.

'What about the rescue swimmer?' Ellis yelled at Kesnick's back.

Maggie heard the howling wind roar through the helicopter. The thump-thump of the rotors and thump-thump of her heartbeat made it difficult to hear the words and she knew it was impossible for Kesnick to hear anything without the communication system inside the helmet.

She held tight to the leather strap, re-adjusted her weight, and shoved herself up onto her feet. Still holding on to the strap, she swiped up Bailey's flight helmet from where she had left it and tapped Kesnick on the shoulder with it. His eyes shot her a look of surprise then he nodded, yanked on the helmet, and adjusted the mike.

'Liz's caught in a crosswind,' Kesnick yelled. 'She's spinning.'

'Son of a bitch,' Wilson answered.

'I'm pulling her back,' Kesnick said, planting his feet.

In seconds Kesnick had Bailey back inside

the helicopter.

Maggie handed Liz her own helmet. Then Maggie sat against the wall, gripping the leather strap with gloved fingers, noticing now how badly her hands were shaking. She could no longer hear the conversation taking place. Both Kesnick and Bailey looked remarkably calm.

It seemed like less than a couple of minutes and Bailey handed the helmet back to Maggie, replacing it with her lighter-weight swim helmet. Maggie checked her eyes in that brief exchange. There was no hesitation. No fear.

Bailey scooted back to the open doorway, waited for Kesnick's tap on the chest, gave him a thumbs-up, and to Maggie's disbelief, the young rescue swimmer rolled out of the helicopter again.

NINETEEN

Platt stared at the dead boy's face. He looked so much younger than the nineteen years recorded on his chart. Stripped of everything, including his life, his gray body appeared small, his prosthetic leg emphasizing his vulnerabilities. It gnawed at Platt to think that this brave kid survived Afghanistan and his battle wounds only to come home and die from some mysterious disease.

Gowned up again, Platt stood beside the stainless-steel autopsy table going over the chart when he realized the pathologist, Dr Anslo, was waiting for him. The man's almost nonexistent eyebrows were raised, their presence distinct only because Anslo's shaved head and smooth face left nothing else to forecast his emotions. His latex-gloved hand were held up in front of him, signaling that he was ready – ready and waiting for this guest who had been imposed on him.

Platt quickly found what he as searching for: the boy's name, Ronald (Ronnie) William Towers. It was a small thing, but he wanted to know how to address this young man, if nowhere else but in his own mind. It was the least he could do. Ronnie Towers deserved that small, last respect.

'I'm ready,' said Platt.

This part of his job always challenged his sensibilities. It didn't help matters that he had just returned from Afghanistan and had witnessed the carnage that young men like Ronnie had to deal with every day of their tours. It battered his psyche as much as the exhaustion did. Each trip to Afghanistan or Iraq reminded Platt why, as an army doctor, he had chosen laboratories filled with vials, test tubes, and glass slides rather than the OR.

'I'll need a vial of his blood.'

Anslo gave a terse nod as though Platt was wasting time telling him something he already knew.

'And a tissue sample.'

'Fine,' Anslo said, shifting his weight in an exaggerated show of impatience as he continued to hold up his hands, waiting for instructions.

'Would you mind starting at the surgical site?' Platt asked.

The man's long, drawn-out sigh told Platt exactly what Anslo thought of his request. He didn't, however, refuse.

'If you tell me what you're looking for, perhaps I could help.'

'I don't know.'

'You don't know?'

'No,' Platt admitted and avoided Anslo's eyes.

Since he arrived, Platt had tried to sift through as many of the files as possible looking for some common thread. All of the injuries had begun as compound bone fractures with deep tissue and bone exposed to open air for an extended period.

Dr Anslo disconnected Ronnie's prosthetic, set it aside, and began on the surgical site just below his knee.

'Everything looks quite normal,' he told Platt without glancing up at him. 'If you're searching for an infection, I don't believe you'll find it here.'

Initially Platt had thought it might be an airborne bacterium. In Iraq he had seen a bone infection called osteomyelitis (OM), prevalent in the Middle East. It often occurred in severe fractures where the bone was left exposed. But OM wasn't fatal or life-threatening. Sometimes, though rarely, it cost a soldier his limb. And sometimes it led to or acted as a primer for *methicillin-resistant Staphylococcus aureus,* MRSA.

Captain Ganz had told Platt there was now a compound, a bone cement pumped full of antibiotics, that allowed them to apply those antibiotics directly to the fracture site, reducing such infections. In addition, Ganz had tested for MRSA. The tests were negative. Platt should have known that it was too easy of an answer.

If not MRSA, Platt wondered, then what? Was it possibly another deadly pathogen that resembled MRSA and was not only resistant to antibiotics but could also lie dormant, hidden inside the cells, waiting for something to trigger it into action? Could a bone infection like OM mutate into something fatal? Given the right ingredients – like an open-air wound, a deep-tissue, bone-exposed wound – anything was possible. Platt had seen it happen before. But not like this. Invisible with no initial symptoms.

Dr Anslo was staring at him again. The

raised eyebrows showing his discontent while he waited for instructions.

'Go ahead,' Platt told him. 'Proceed with your normal routine.' But before Dr. Anslo began the Y incision down Ronnie Towers's chest, Platt said to him, 'Do you mind if I take this for twenty-four hours.' He pointed at Ronnie's prosthetic.

'You want to take his leg?' This time Anslo didn't need a facial expression to show his disgust. His voice did it for him.

Without apology, Platt said, 'Yes. Would that be okay?'

'I'll have the diener help you fill out the necessary form. May I proceed?' He pointed his chin toward his hands waiting over the boy's chest.

Platt nodded. As a medical doctor, cutting into live tissue was lifesaving. Cutting into dead tissue seemed … such a waste. He was relieved when Anslo turned his back to him so he couldn't see Platt wince.

TWENTY

Liz felt the adrenaline kick in again. The wind continued to whip at her. It took Kesnick three attempts to deploy her within reach of the fishing cruiser. Once, the wind shoved her over it. The second time her toes brushed the rail before the waves swept the tilted deck and the boat out of reach. The whole time she kept her eye on the dog, making sure it didn't decide to protect its master by attacking her. The dog, however, just watched.

The third time a wave crested and shoved the boat up to meet her. Liz kicked her feet out, twisting and jerking her body until she touched the deck. She prayed that her flippers didn't trip her as she caught the slippery railing with her heels just as Kesnick loosened the deployment cable. She slid down between the tilted deck and the railing.

The dog had stayed put, watching his master, almost pointing his nose into the water. His eyes followed Liz. Despite the howl of the wind and the crash of the waves she thought she could hear the dog moan. That's when she noticed the second dog inside the cabin. From the helicopter, the roof had hidden his existence. He was larger than the first dog but his weight didn't cause a shift. He paced back and forth, following the natural sway of the disabled boat.

Liz kept herself from glancing up at the helicopter. No sense in telegraphing this problem too early.

Kesnick gave more slack for her to maneuver over the sinking boat. She knew her extra weight could capsize it. She crawled slowly toward the man. He wasn't moving. It wasn't until she was within five feet that she saw his eyes watching her. A good sign. Shock hadn't completely debilitated him.

His arm draped over the railing was the only thing that prevented him from floating away from the boat, but it lay at an odd angle. He wasn't hanging on. He was caught, the arm most likely broken. It must have happened when he flipped overboard, keeping him out of the water from the waist up. That is, when the waves weren't crushing his legs against the boat.

When Liz could safely reach out without further tilting the deck, she grabbed on to his life jacket. His eyes grew wider. The slight movement had reminded him of the pain. She wouldn't be able to use the quick strop on him. The harness was meant to fit under the survivor's arms. She'd need them to deploy the basket. She took a cable hooked to her belt and started to wind it around the man's waist. If nothing else, it would prevent him from getting sucked under the boat if it capsized.

Then she waved up at the helicopter, giving the signal to send down the basket. This, too, presented a challenge. The winds swept the basket in every direction but down to Liz. They couldn't put it in the water for the same reason she had attached the cable to the man's waist. The basket could get sucked under. Kesnick would need to place it right on the deck, steadying it with the cable so it didn't add weight to the boat.

This took several tries.

'I'm not going without my dogs,' the man told Liz as she wrestled him up.

'I've been told the dogs can't go. They'll need to wait for the cutter.'

He shoved at her, wincing at the pain in his arm. 'Then I'll wait with them.'

Again, Liz avoided glancing up at the helicopter. Had they seen him push her away? They might just think she hurt him.

'Either one of them a biter?' she asked.

He was silent and she knew immediately that he didn't want to condemn one or the other.

'Sir, you're gonna have to trust me.'

'He only did it once and he was defending me.'

'This one,' she said turning her head, avoiding any gestures the helicopter crew might interpret.

'Yeah, Benny.'

'And the other one?'

'He's a big baby. Can't you tell?' he said with a smile, but it disappeared when he said, 'I didn't buy them life jackets. I can't believe I thought I'd save a couple of bucks.' He shook his head, biting his lip. But it wasn't pain this time. It was regret. 'You can't leave them. Please.'

Liz guessed the guy was in his forties, small-framed – thank God – and an amateur fisherman. Later she'd ask if the boat was new, perhaps a splurge. His foolish attempt at recreation had almost cost him his life. And now she knew it might very well cost her own neck.

TWENTY-ONE

Maggie slid into a position close enough to the open doorway that she could watch Bailey. Whatever the woman had given her earlier seemed to be helping. She wasn't nauseated; however, her stomach dived every time Bailey plunged. It didn't matter that the rescue swimmer was attached to the helicopter by a cable. Each attempt to drop her onto the boat looked more like a circus stunt gone horribly wrong.

Kesnick relayed every move step-by-step to his other two crew members. Minutes ago he said there might be a problem.

'The guy's refusing to get into the basket.'

'From what I've heard,' Ellis said, 'she was able to talk her way around some real crazies in New Orleans after Katrina.'

'What do mean, talk her way around?' Wilson wanted to know.

'You heard about some of the situations. The crew would hover down over a flooded area where a couple of people were stranded, and as soon as the rescue swimmer got down there other people swarmed out demanding rescue. Some nasty dudes, too. I guess Bailey had to tell them women and children or injured got first priority. They didn't much like it.'

'So what happened?'

'She said what she needed to, to get them to listen to her.'

'Humph.'

Maggie glanced over at Wilson. His grunt sounded like he wasn't impressed.

'She's getting him in the basket,' Kesnick announced.

'All right.' Ellis pumped a fist.

'It's about time. Pull him up,' Wilson told him.

'No signal yet.'

More minutes ticked by and then Maggie realized what Bailey was up to right about the same time Kesnick did. She saw him glance back at his pilot as if looking for a way to not report what was going on below.

'What's the holdup?' Wilson wanted to know.

No answer.

'Kesnick, what the hell's going on?'

'I think she's bringing the dog up with the guy.'

'She's not bringing up that dog, Kesnick.' Wilson's anger rocked the controls and the helicopter jerked to the right.

'She's putting the dog in on top of the guy.'

'You have got to be kidding me,' Ellis yelled, but Maggie thought it sounded like he was smiling.

'I told her not to bring up that dog.'

Maggie saw Bailey wave the all clear and up, and Kesnick didn't hesitate. He concentrated on raising the basket, keeping it steady. Maggie watched Bailey down below. She had crawled back farther onto the deck, under the cabin roof.

Kesnick pulled and yanked, getting the basket into the helicopter's cabin, sliding and grinding it over the entry. The whole time his attention was focused on the survivor and the dog. Maggie knew Kesnick hadn't even seen the second dog that Bailey had dragged from the cabin. She had it clutched tight to her chest and managed to harness it to her safety belt.

'Son of a bitch,' Kesnick said as he grasped the deployment cable.

'What now?' Wilson asked.

Maggie glanced between Wilson and Kesnick while watching the survivor settle against the cabin wall, hugging what looked like a broken arm. The dog stayed close to his owner, panting and licking the man's hand. Maggie was glad he couldn't hear the exchange between Kesnick and Wilson.

'There's a second dog,' Kesnick finally admitted.

'She better not be bringing up another dog.'

'She's bringing up the second dog.'

'Don't raise that dog up.'

'She has it in the quick strop. She's holding it.'

'Son of a bitch. Don't raise her up, Kesnick. Leave her butt down there until she puts that damn dog back.'

Maggie watched Kesnick's face, the half she could see below his eye shield. She thought she saw a hint of a smile. What Wilson didn't realize and couldn't see was that the flight mechanic already had Bailey halfway up. She was almost to the helicopter.

TWENTY-TWO

Walter Bailey flipped over the open sign on his Coney Island Canteen. It was later than he'd like. Sundays were big days for him, but he'd promised his daughter Liz that he'd get gasoline first. He'd gotten extra and took a couple of five-gallon canisters to his other

112

daughter, Trish. As he'd suspected, his son-in-law, Scott, hadn't even thought about preparing for the hurricane. Trish, as always, defended her husband.

'He's from Michigan, Dad. He has no idea what a hurricane means.'

'He'll learn quickly. This one is on its way.'

Walter hadn't really believed that when he said it. But it made him mad that Scott chose to 'run into work' – as Trish put it – instead of helping his wife prepare. It was a father's overprotective instinct kicking in, but he didn't like Scott Larsen. Sometimes that slipped out. Lately he didn't care. Trish deserved better. Though everyone believed this young man was a charming, hardworking, devoted husband, Walter saw beyond the veneer. Maybe it was just Scott's profession that annoyed Walter. In his mind, morticians were just better-dressed salesmen.

By the time Walter got to Pensacola Beach, the winds had kicked up and surfers were riding the waves. It was what Walter liked to call 'beatin' down' hot, not a strip of shade or cool around.

He had a line of customers before the first set of dogs were ready, but Walter enjoyed chatting and could make his hot, hungry customers laugh and share stories. His career as a navy pilot and commander not only made for good entertainment but also had trained him well in convincing people

113

that his mission was their mission. They weren't just buying a hot dog and Coke from the Coney Island Canteen, they were paying tribute to Walter's boyhood. Okay, so perhaps the salesman in him simply recognized the salesman in Scott.

The crowd thinned out, finally replaced by a young guy – no more than thirty. Neat, short-cropped hair. Dressed in khaki walking shorts, a purple polo shirt – though Walter's wife would have corrected him and called it lavender – and Sperry deck shoes. Walter's wife had taught him how to dress. After thirty-five years of wearing a uniform he had no idea who Ralph Lauren was. But now he did and recognized the logo on the lavender shirt. He noticed other details, too – like the gold Rolex and Ray-Bans – without showing that he noticed. The guy was probably not a tourist. Maybe a businessman. He didn't look like he knew anything about boats, though Walter had seen better-dressed amateurs step off some of the yachts in the marina. It was ridiculous what people thought they needed to wear these days, even for recreation.

'What can I get on it?' the guy asked.

'Just about anything you want.'

'Green peppers?'

'Sure. Green peppers, kraut, onions.'

Walter thought he recognized the guy but couldn't place him.

'All of that sounds good. Add some mustard and relish. So what's with the Coney Island getup? You from New York?'

'Nope. Pennsylvania. But my daddy took us to Coney Island a couple of times for vacation. Those were some of the best days. You been to Coney Island?'

'No. But my dad talked about it. Where in Pennsylvania?'

'Upper Darby.'

'Get out. Really?'

Walter stopped with a forkful of kraut to look at the guy. 'You know Upper Darby?'

'My dad grew up in Philadelphia. He talked about Upper Darby.'

'Is that right?' Walter finished, wrapped the hot dog in a napkin, nestled it into a paper dish, and handed it to the guy. 'Would I know him? Where'd he go to high school?'

'You know, I'm not sure. He died a few years ago. Cancer. His name was Phillip Norris. He didn't stay in Philadelphia. Joined the navy.'

'Retired navy,' Walter said, pointing a thumb to his chest.

'No kidding?' The guy took a careful bite of the hot dog, nodded, and smiled. 'This is one good dog.'

'One hundred percent beef.'

'Hey, Mr. B,' a scrawny kid interrupted.

'Danny, my boy. Ready for your regular?'

'Yes, sir.'

115

'Danny here is quite the entrepreneur.' Walter always tried to bring his customers together.

'Is that right?'

'Working on the beach cleanup crew and living out of his car to save money.'

'And to surf,' Danny added.

'His surfboard is worth more than his car.'

Danny shrugged and smiled. Walter knew the boy enjoyed the attention. He wasn't sure what the kid's story was. He looked about fifteen but Walter had seen his driver's license and it listed him at eighteen and from someplace in Kansas. Maybe the kid really did just want to surf.

Danny had the routine down. Worked the cleanup crew in the evenings till about eleven, slept in his car, surfed all day, used the outdoor showers on the beach and the public rest-rooms on the boardwalk, ate hot dogs with mustard, onion, and kraut with a Coke. Not a bad life, Walter supposed.

He handed the kid his hot dog and poured an extra-large Coke, then accepted the boy's two bucks. Their agreement. Walter figured this was the kid's only real meal of the day, so he cut him a deal.

Another line started forming. A bunch of college kids, pushing and shoving at one another.

While handing Walter a ten-dollar bill, Norris was watching Danny get into his faded red Impala. Maybe the kid reminded him of himself.

'On the house,' Walter said.

That got his attention.

'I can't let you do that.' The guy looked stunned like no one had ever said that to him before. 'Besides, I can more than afford it,' he said, swinging his head and his eyes back in Danny's direction.

'I know you can. Come back and buy one tomorrow. That one's on me. For your daddy – one vet to another. Now go enjoy. You're holding up my traffic.'

Norris wandered off to the side, glancing at the people behind him. The ten-dollar bill stayed in his hand like he didn't know what to do with it. He thought he might have offended the guy. That he might stick around and try to pay him again.

Walter wished he could figure out what was so familiar about him, even though the name Phillip Norris didn't ring any bells. He realized he should ask where his dad was stationed in the navy. But when he looked up the guy was gone.

TWENTY-THREE

Scott Larsen ignored his ringing cell phone. It was either a grieving family calling to nag or it was Trish, and he didn't want to talk to her, either. After a quick glance he continued through the hotel lobby. It was Trish. She didn't appreciate him leaving again, even if it was for business. She'd gotten herself worked up about this frickin' hurricane. He was getting so tired of everybody worrying about this storm when there wasn't a cloud in the sky.

Trish had probably remembered one more thing to harangue him about. Something else her daddy had done for her.

'Daddy brought us some gasoline,' she had told him earlier.

'Wow. He spent his entire week's hot-dog money.'

'That's rude. He was being gracious.'

'Taking care of his little girl.'

'Maybe he thought he had to because her husband wasn't doing a very good job.'

'I'm off making a living. Paying the bills.'

'If this hurricane hits, none of that will matter.'

And by this time she had worked herself

into angry tears, which automatically clicked Scott into his professional comforter role. He'd put an arm around her shoulder, instigated the combination hand pat while whispering a series of soothing words and phrases.

By the time she spoke again the hitch in her voice was gone. 'I guess we just have to hope our insurance covers everything.'

That knocked Scott cold. No way he could tell her now that he hadn't taken out insurance on their new place, the dream house that had already skyrocketed over their budget and would almost be finished if his wife would quit changing and adding.

'Daddy said we can stay with him during the hurricane. We can't stay here on the bay. We'll be safe at Daddy's.'

By then Scott hadn't been listening anymore except to the key words that irritated him. Words like 'daddy.' Southern girls sure did love their daddies. Scott would never get used to that term of endearment. Not from a grown woman. Daddy was what a five-year-old called his father.

Trish had pouted a little while he changed clothes but didn't say much more before he left. His Midwest work ethic was one characteristic she found appealing after all the deadbeats she'd dated. Besides he promised he'd help her board up the patio doors at their new house in the morning as long as they were finished by noon. He had to move up a memorial service for a stiff in his fridge. The family had originally scheduled for Wednesday but now they were all freaked about the hurricane and wanted to bury Uncle Mel before the storm hit.

Promising to help board up had seemed to satisfy Trish. So maybe she wasn't calling just to nag at him. He pulled out his cell phone as he sat down at the hotel's deck bar. He was just about to listen to Trish's voice message when the blond bartender appeared in front of him.

'Your friend's already here,' she told him with a smile. 'He said to tell you to meet him inside the restaurant. He's buying you dinner.'

'Really?' But Scott was more impressed with the attention she was paying him than the dinner invitation.

'Why don't you guys stop out here later for a drink,' she said, then hurried across the bar to wait on another customer.

Her smile made him forget why he had his cell phone out and he simply slipped it back into his shirt pocket. As he headed into the restaurant he vowed to assuage all the stress of the day. Assuage. Yes, that was a cool word, one that Joe Black would probably use. Scott decided he'd find a way to use it in their conversation.

TWENTY-FOUR

Maggie's knees felt weak. Her ears still hummed and if she looked, she knew she'd see a slight tremor in her fingers. But she was relieved to be back on the ground, away from the thumping rotors and the nerve-rattling vibration.

Escambia County sheriff Joshua Clayton was waiting for her, and everything about his tall, lanky body – from his tapping toe to his erratic gesturing – told Maggie that he wasn't happy. But he'd promised Charlie Wurth that the DHS and FBI would have full disclosure of the evidence. Clayton didn't seem to have a problem with allowing access. It was his time he had a problem sparing, and at one point he mumbled, 'I don't have time for this. There's a hurricane on its way, for Christ's sake.'

Maggie had barely peeled out of her flight suit. She thanked the aircrew and they agreed to meet later for drinks on her. Clayton stood at her elbow the entire time, twisting his wrist in an exaggerated show of checking the time. Now, in his cruiser, the man was tapping out his impatience on the steering wheel.

Back at the office he handed her a form to

121

sign then led her to a small room at the end of a hallway. There was nothing on the walls. Only a table and two folding chairs sat on the worn but clean linoleum. On the table was the battered white fishing cooler.

'Contents were photographed and bagged,' Clayton told her. 'They're all at the ME's office. We haven't processed the cooler yet,' he said as he handed her a pair of latex gloves. 'We'll dust it for prints, but with it being in the water I suspect we won't find much.'

His cell phone rang. Clayton frowned at it.

'I've got to take this. You mind?'

'Go ahead.'

He was out the door in three strides. Maggie couldn't help but notice that despite his initial frown, he looked relieved to have a reason to escape. His voice disappeared down the hallway. It was just as well. She preferred taking a close look without him standing over her shoulder.

She began opening the lid but snapped it shut after just a whiff of the rancid smell. She prepared herself, took a deep breath, and tried again. No wonder they hadn't processed the cooler yet. About two inches of pink liquid covered the bottom, residue from melted ice and at least one leaky package.

Maggie let the lid flap open. The initial smell would be the worst. Adding some air would dilute it. She stepped away and pulled her smartphone from its holder at her waistband. She pushed a couple buttons and activated the camera.

The cooler was huge, white paint over stainless steel. A popular name brand that even Maggie recognized was stamped on the side. The inside of the lid was unusual, with an indentation of a large fish and slots of measurement alongside it. What drew her immediate attention was the tie-down, looped around the cooler's handle.

She took several pictures, close-ups to focus on the blue-and-yellow twisted strands. The rope was made of synthetic fiber, smooth, possibly coated. One end appeared to be frayed. She took more pictures. On closer inspection it looked like the frayed end had been cut, not ripped. All the fibers, though frayed, were the exact same length.

Maggie glanced back at the door. No sight or sound of Sheriff Clayton. But, just in case, she chose to text-message her partner, R. J. Tully, rather than make a phone call.

HEY TULLY. SENDING PHOTOS.
CAN U CHECK DATABASE?

It took her less than a minute to e-mail close-ups of the rope. Tully would be able to scan or download the photos and run the information through the FBI's database. Maybe they'd get lucky and be able to identify the manufacturer.

She remembered another case in the 1980s. An airman named John Joubert was arrested for murdering two little boys. Authorities found an unusual rope at one of the crime scenes. It had been used to bind the hands of one of the boys. This was before DNA analysis, so the unusual rope became a key piece of evidence. During a search of Joubert's quarters, they found a length of it.

Before she sent the last photo she had a text message from Tully.

NO PROB.

Finished with the rope, she moved on and shot photos of the cooler and the measuring tool inside the lid. Not much to see. She agreed with Sheriff Clayton's speculations about fingerprints. Maybe they'd get lucky with a print inside the lid, but the salt water had probably eliminated anything on the outside.

Maggie took a final shot of the open cooler, the smell less potent now. That's when she noticed something in the liquid. She held her breath again and leaned over for a closer look. A small piece of white paper, no larger than two inches by three inches, was stuck to the side, several inches from the bottom. Part of the paper fell below the liquid's surface and the moisture had loosened a corner. Had it not been for it flapping into the liquid, Maggie would have never noticed. And that was probably why Sheriff Clayton's staff had missed it.

She glanced over her shoulder. As she holstered her smart-phone she searched the room. In a lone cupboard behind the door she found a box of ziplock bags. She grabbed one and pulled on the latex gloves Clayton had given her. Then carefully and slowly she peeled the piece of paper from the cooler wall, trying to limit her touch to the flapping corner as she eased it off little by little.

Maggie held the paper between her finger-tips. She needed to be patient and let it air-dry before placing it into the plastic bag. As she waited she examined the other side of the paper. Its corners were rounded, resembling a stick-on label. The side that had been facing out was blank but the one that had been stuck to the wall of the cooler was not. The ink had bled away. Only a ghost of the hand printing remained. But Maggie could still read the three lines of letters and numbers, what looked like a code:

AMET
DESTIN: 082409
#8509000029

She glanced back inside the cooler. There was nothing else. Maybe this piece of paper didn't have a thing to do with the body parts. It could have been left over from the cooler's previous usage. Perhaps dropped in accidentally.

Or, and Maggie hoped this was the case, it had once been a label attached to one of the packages.

TWENTY-FIVE

Benjamin Platt leaned his elbows on the lab countertop. He pressed his eyes against the microscope and adjusted the magnification. Once in a while he glanced up at the test tubes he had prepared, watching for the results. Ronnie Towers's blood had already tested negative for several of Platt's best guesses. He was running out of ideas.

The small laboratory suited him despite the strong smell of disinfectants. It was well equipped and quiet, much better than the conditions he was used to on the road. Platt had learned long ago to travel with a hard-shell case filled with everything he'd need to run basic lab tests whether he was in a war zone, a hot zone, or even a tent in Sierra Leone.

He sat back on the stool and stared at the test tubes. No change. A good thing, albeit frustrating as hell. The young man's prosthetic leg rested on the counter next to him. He had carefully scraped some of the bone paste applied to the prosthetic during surgery. He smeared it on a slide then prepared a second slide from the sample tissue taken from Ronnie Towers.

What he had found so far was something he identified as a strain of *Clostridia,* a family of bacteria that caused a number of infections. The most prevalent one was tetanus. Another was sepsis leading to toxic shock syndrome. Except what Platt saw under the microscope looked more complicated.

To his left, Platt had opened his laptop, accessing a database he had worked for several years to put together. Now on the screen was a close-up of the *Clostridia* family. He needed to wait for all the files to download before he could begin clicking through the photos in his database. He hoped he would find an exact match to what he saw under his microscope.

While he waited, he pulled out his cell phone. Certainly he could get some basic information without breaking his word to Captain Ganz about keeping this situation classified.

He keyed in the number, expecting to get the voice-messaging service for the Centers for Disease Control's chief of outbreak response. Platt was surprised when Roger Bix's slow, Southern drawl answered, 'This is Bix.'

'Roger, it's Benjamin Platt.'

'Colonel, what can I do for you?'

'I didn't expect to get you on a Sunday.'

'It's a 24/7 job.' He laughed. 'I doubt you're calling me from a golf course. What's up?'

'I'm wondering if you have any recent reports of life-threatening infections related to ... say, any kind of donor tissue or bone transplants?'

'Illnesses, sure. Deaths? None if your definition of recent is the last forty-eight hours. I'd have to check for sure. Are you calling to report one?'

Platt had forgotten how direct and to the point Bix could be. Not a bad thing. The last time the two men had worked together they were dealing with two separate outbreaks of Ebola.

'Just need information,' Platt told him. 'If there was a possible contamination at a tissue bank or a hospital, you'd know, right?'

'Depends what the contamination is. Tissue banks are required to screen donors for HIV, hepatitis B and C, and other blood-borne viruses.'

'What about bacteria?'

'What kind of bacteria?'

'I don't know, Roger.' He felt himself shrugging as he stared at his computer screen. 'Infection-causing bacterium.'

'The FDA doesn't require us to culture donors for anything beyond blood-borne viruses. Many of the accredited tissue banks don't go beyond those requirements. Infections are rare. I won't say they never happen. I remember several years back three deaths in Minnesota. Routine knee surgeries using the cartilage from a cadaver. But that was a freaky case. Even our investigation couldn't determine whether the donor was already infected or whether the tissue became infected while it was processed. The tissue bank blamed the collection agency and the collection agency blamed the shipper. It's a crazy business.'

'Business?'

'Sure. It's a business. Organ transplants have strict regulations. Only one organization per region. Have to be nonprofit, so plenty of federal oversight. Whole different ball game. But you get into tissue, bone, ligaments, corneas, veins – the supply can't keep up with demand. A cadaver might be worth $5,000 to $10,000, but sliced and diced – excuse my flippancy – and sold piece by piece? That same cadaver's worth anywhere from $25,000 to $40,000.'

'I thought it was illegal to sell cadavers and human body parts.'

'Ben, no offense, but man, you need to get out of the lab more often. Selling body parts might be illegal but it's not illegal to charge for the service of procuring, processing, and transporting. But truthfully, a lot of good comes out of this stuff. Some of the technology is amazing. They say one donor – by using his bones, tissue, ligaments, skin – can affect fifty lives.'

Platt felt his stomach sink to his knees. One donor could *infect* fifty recipients?

'Ben, I hope you're not working on another fiasco that the military is trying to keep quiet.'

'No, of course not.'

Platt was glad Roger Bix didn't know him well, or he'd recognize what a terrible liar he was.

TWENTY-SIX

Scott downed his Johnnie Walker – neat, this time – trying to keep up with Joe Black. Maybe he'd get used to the sting. His head started to spin. It wasn't unpleasant. In fact, he sort of liked the feeling. It didn't even bother him when Joe cut into his rare steak and the red juices leaked out and streamed across his bone-white plate, soaking into his baked potato.

Joe had ordered a bottle of wine for them to share with their porterhouses and Scott noticed he was a bit behind on the wine. Joe was pouring a second glass for himself and topping off Scott's. And the whole time Scott couldn't shake out of his mind the envelope Joe had handed him when they first sat down. It would have been uncool to pull the money out, but with only a glance Scott saw the envelope contained hundred-dollar bills. And there were certainly more than the five hundred dollars they had agreed on.

'Your finder's fee for the indie,' Joe smiled at him. 'And a little extra for the storage space I'm going to need. Looks like the conference is being postponed. I have some frozen specimens I'll need to bring in. So are we good?'

'Oh, absolutely. Other than what we added earlier, I only have one guy in there now and the family wants the service Tuesday morning. Not even an open casket. They wanna get the old coot buried before the storm hits.'

'And you're set up with generators, just in case?'

'All set,' Scott told him and made a mental note in the back of his spinning head to check.

'I have a delivery coming in tomorrow morning,' Joe told him. 'I asked them to re-route it to the funeral home. You'll be there around ten, right?'

'Absolutely. Not a problem.'

'How old of a guy?'

'Excuse me?'

'The old coot.'

'Oh, him. Sixty-nine. Bachelor. Lived alone.'

'Obese?'

Scott stopped mid-bite. Even with a fuzzy head, Joe's interest seemed odd.

Joe noticed Scott's hesitancy and said, 'Just curious,' and sipped his wine. 'You know how it is. Occupational hazard.' He gave Scott one of his winning grins and Scott relaxed.

'You should hear the calls I get,' Joe continued. 'Independent brokers, toolers, even surgeons contact me. And the worst are these conference organizers. You should hear them. "Hey, Joe, I need six torsos, five shoulders, and a dozen knee specimens in two weeks."'

He slung back the rest of his wine, reached for the bottle, and filled his glass, taking time to top off Scott's again.

'And you should see these conferences.' Joe pushed his plate aside and planted an elbow in its place on the table. 'Five-star resorts, usually with beaches and golf courses. First-class flight, deluxe suite, dinners, cocktail parties. It's all included for the surgeons.'

Scott slid his plate aside and mirrored Joe's posture, leaning in and sipping his wine. He really didn't need any more alcohol. His head was already starting to swim. But now he just nodded and listened, grateful because he wasn't sure he could trust his words to not slur.

'And for guys like us, Scott? The sky's the limit. Don't get me wrong. I respect the rules of the trade. It's not my fault there're so few. And as long as I transport within Florida I don't even have to worry about shipping regulations.'

Scott was still stuck on the phrase 'guys like us.' He liked that Joe finally considered him a part of his network, his 'hood.

'Can I get you gentlemen some dessert?'

The waitress's sudden presence startled Scott.

'Yes,' Joe answered as smoothly as if he hadn't had several Scotches and half a bottle of wine. 'How 'bout the flaming cherries jubilee?' He was asking Scott, not the waitress.

'Oh, absolutely,' Scott managed, surprised at sounding so coherent.

'Excellent choice.' She rewarded Joe with a smile.

'Oh, and I need to get a cheeseburger to go. Medium well,' he told the waitress.

'Fries?'

'That'd be perfect.'

As she left, Scott raised an eyebrow at Joe. 'Still hungry?'

'Don't ask. I promised someone.'

But something had changed in Joe's demeanor. Scott saw it immediately, though he couldn't put his finger on what it was exactly. It made Joe sit up. He waved a hand over the table.

'This is the lifestyle, Scott. And it only promises to grow. I can't keep up with the demand. Having a few choice funeral directors like yourself has really helped. You know, you guys are the true gatekeepers of America's donor program. You have such tremendous influence over whether a family recognizes the valuable gift their loved one can give to future generations.'

Scott recognized the switch and he felt disappointed. Joe had lapsed back into his 'you guys' pitch. Before the waitress interrupted, it was 'guys like us.' He felt like Joe had started to open up, that they were more like buddies, not the Death Salesman shoring up the ranks.

Once again, Scott wondered who Joe Black really was.

TWENTY-SEVEN

When Maggie offered to buy the aircrew drinks, she honestly didn't think they would show up. It was late. Maybe she should have offered dinner. Food had been the last thing on her mind after a second landing at Baptist Hospital to deliver the injured boater and his two dogs. Now, despite having examined the rancid cooler, she found herself hungry.

While she waited, she checked her phone messages. The Escambia County medical examiner would be processing the body parts at nine tomorrow morning. He gave Maggie directions.

She text-messaged Wurth to join them for drinks, to be her backup, but his quick response was:

Prob not happenin. Catch ya at brkfst?

Maggie hated deciphering text messages. Still none from Tully and she had to remind herself that it was Sunday. Identifying the rope wasn't a matter of life and death. It was just one of those things that nagged at her. When the aircrew arrived, they sat down around her at the table as though meeting an inquisition.

'Just one question,' Maggie told them. 'I promise. Have any of you ever seen a tie-down like that on a fishing cooler?'

'Commercial fishermen use a stainless-steel contraption.' It was Tommy Ellis who answered. 'One end hooks into the cooler, the other into the floor of the boat. There's a turnbuckle in the middle to tighten it. I noticed this cooler had a pre-molded slot for it. A marine professional would use something like that, something more secure and certainly more sophisticated than a rope, even an unusual rope.'

Everyone at the table was staring at Ellis by the time he finished, like he had just revealed some long-hidden secret.

'What?' Ellis shrugged. 'My uncle's a shrimper.'

After one drink Kesnick called it quits. He needed to get home to his wife and kids. The pilots, Wilson and Ellis, had another but then gravitated to the beach bar next door.

'We'll be right back,' they said after spotting someone they knew.

From the look of things Maggie didn't expect them to return anytime soon. She didn't mind. And Liz Bailey looked much more comfortable with her crew gone. She had showered and her short hair, still damp in the humidity, was sticking up in places. She wore khaki shorts and a white sleeveless shirt. Maggie couldn't help thinking that the clothes were fitted just enough to remind Liz's crew she really wasn't one of them. Maggie remembered the discussion back in the helicopter. The men strategizing the rescue and leaving out the opinion of its chief architect – the rescue swimmer.

'This is a new aircrew for you,' Maggie said to Liz.

'That obvious?'

'Not really,' she said, realizing she might sound presumptuous. She wiped at the condensation on the bottle of beer she'd been nursing for the last half hour. She wanted to guzzle it. The air was stifling and it was long past sundown. 'I get paid the big bucks to figure out psychological stuff like that.'

She was pleased to see Liz Bailey smile for the first time since they'd met.

'What do you expect when you put four type-A personalities together in a heli-copter. It's okay, though,' Liz said, pausing to take a sip of her beer. 'By now I'm used to having to prove myself.'

'For what it's worth, they were really worried about you.'

'Really?'

'Yes, really.'

'When they were worried, what did they

call me?'

'What do you mean?'

'Did they say, "How's Bailey?" Or "Is the rescue swimmer okay?"'

'Yes,' Maggie told her. 'They wanted to know if the rescue swimmer was okay.'

'Yeah. That's what I thought.' She took a long unladylike swig from her bottle while Maggie waited for some sort of explanation. Finally Liz said, 'You're the psychology expert. Even after today's rescue they're still calling me *the* rescue swimmer, not *our* rescue swimmer. What does that tell you?'

Maggie detected disappointment more than anger in Liz's voice, despite her attempt at humor.

'It tells me they're men.'

This time Liz laughed and tipped her bottle to Maggie as a salute of agreement. 'You got that right.'

'Not to change the subject' – though it was the subject of male-female camaraderie that reminded Maggie – 'but what was that you gave me before the flight? The capsules?'

'Did they work?'

'Yes, and believe me, I've tried everything.'

'It's powdered ginger.'

'Ginger? You're kidding?'

'Works wonders for the nausea. Doesn't make a difference what's causing the nausea, this squelches it. So what is it?'

'Excuse me?'

'What caused it? Your nausea?' Her eyes found Maggie's and held them. 'I mean you're an FBI agent. You carry a gun. Someone said you're like this expert profiler of murderers. I imagine you've seen some stuff that could turn plenty of cast-iron stomachs. But being up in the air. It's about something else?'

Maggie caught herself shrugging and then felt a bit silly under the scrutiny of this young woman. After all, earlier Liz had seen that there was a problem when Maggie thought for certain she had learned to hide it.

'Hey, it's none of my business. Just making conversation,' Liz told her and looked away like it was no big deal.

But after what they had just gone through in the helicopter, not to mention sneaking the gift of the capsules to Maggie – who kept almost everyone she met at a safe distance – she felt Liz deserved an answer.

'I'm sure it does seem odd,' Maggie finally said. 'You're right, I've seen plenty of things: body parts stuffed into takeout containers, little boys carved up. Just yesterday I had to pluck a killer's brains out of my hair.' She checked Liz's face and was surprised none of this fazed her. Then Maggie remembered the guys talking about Bailey and Hurricane Katrina. 'You've seen plenty of stuff, too.'

Another smile. This one totally unexpected.

'You really are very good at this psychology stuff,' Liz said.

Maggie winced. She hadn't intentionally meant to deflect the question.

'I don't think it's that big of a mystery,' Maggie said. 'I can't handle not being in control.'

'Are you always in control when you face off against a killer?'

'Of course. I carry a gun.' Back to brevity and humor. Keep it light, she told herself. Someone gets too close, resort to wit.

'Or maybe in the air you're just vulnerable enough to realize all the risks you take every single day on the ground.'

Maggie stared at her, suddenly disarmed.

'Come on, let's walk.' Liz stood and pointed to the moonlit beach. 'If Isaac hits, this might be the last time we enjoy Pensacola Beach for a very long time.'

Just as Maggie pushed off her barstool a man stumbled over to their table, grabbing the edge and jiggling the empty beer bottles.

'Hey, E-liz-a-beth.' He purposely enunciated her name, stringing it out in his inebriated attempt at song.

'Scott?'

'Oh hey.' He stopped himself when he saw Maggie, as if only then noticing there was someone else at the table. 'Sorry.' He grinned, looking from Liz to Maggie and back. 'I didn't realize you were on a date.'

TWENTY-EIGHT

'Stryker's a 3.96 billion dollar a year company,' Captain Ganz said.

Platt listened, though his eyes stayed on the prosthetic leg as he manipulated the joints.

'Most people know the name Stryker from autopsy scenes in crime novels or on *CSI*. You know, Stryker bone saws? But the company's been an innovator for years when it comes to medical technology. Most hospital surgical beds are even made by Stryker.'

'What about these?' Platt poked at several screws on a table beside him. 'I've never seen anything like them.'

'The technology isn't all that new. We use a company in Jacksonville called BIOMedics. They're able to grind the screws from bone – I guess they call it precision tooling. And they don't just do screws – chips, wedges, dowels, anchors. The human body accepts bone much more readily than plastic. Same theory as heart valves and using animal tissue versus mechanical implants. BIOMedics makes the bone paste we use, too.'

'Paste? You mentioned bone cement earlier.'

'Right. Cement, paste – they're similar. We use the cement to anchor a prosthetic limb. The paste fills the cracks or perforations that might be in the remaining bone. For instance, gaps left by shrapnel. If you fill the holes, bacterium doesn't have as many places to infect.'

'Sort of like medical caulk?'

Ganz laughed. 'I suppose you could make that comparison.' He sipped his third cup of coffee since the two had taken up residence in his office. 'Both the cement and paste have been lifesavers. I told you about it reducing *Staph* infections. We inject antibiotics into the cement and paste. Lets us apply doses directly to the site. Keeps the patients from having to have their bodies blasted with antibiotics, reducing the immune system.'

'What are the chances of it being contaminated?'

'The bone paste?'

'The cement, the paste, the screws. Perhaps the original bone they're made from?' Platt asked, picking up one of the screws and examining it.

Ganz shook his head. 'No, I'd say that's next to impossible. We use our own.'

'What do you mean, you use your own?'

'We have our own supply of bone and tissue.'

Platt didn't bother to hide his surprise.

'The navy was the first to use frozen bone

142

transplants,' Ganz explained. 'Back in the forties at the Naval Medical Center in Maryland. An orthopedic surgeon by the name of Hyatt started freezing and storing bones that he'd surgically removed during amputation. Instead of discarding the bone he'd freeze it, store it, and use what he could to repair fractures in other patients. Sorry,' Ganz interrupted himself. 'Don't mean to give you a history lesson.'

'I don't mind. Go on.'

'Hyatt was so successful he started one of the first body-donation programs. That's how the Navy Tissue Bank started. Even back then they were able to remove more than just bone – tissue, veins, skin, corneas – though they weren't quite sure what to do with most of it. They offered surgeons free use of the bank, only asking that they share their results so Hyatt and his colleagues could maintain their database. It was all pretty much trial and error, but Hyatt figured out a way to disinfect and screen the tissue. Even developed a way to freeze-dry it for shipping. The operation we have today is much more focused and we limit it only to military surgeons.'

'Where does the bone and tissue get processed?'

'In Jacksonville. I recommended Dr. McCleary, the pathologist. He came out of retirement just to run the program. Does an amazing job with the aid of only one diener.'

'So you ship him your ... bones? Your excess...?'

Ganz nodded and smiled at Platt's loss of terminology. 'It's part of the program I started here.'

'Why not do all of it here?'

'Jacksonville had a well-equipped facility already available. Plus it's practically next door to BIOMedics, the company that does all the precision tooling.'

'Who does the screening and disinfecting?'

'Dr. McCleary does it with the help of BIOMedics. I know what you're thinking, Ben. I've already considered contamination. We've checked and double-checked. We've never had a problem before.'

'Have you checked any of the precision-tooled stuff from the dead soldiers?'

Ganz's hesitation gave Platt his answer.

'No,' Ganz finally said. 'I don't believe we removed any of it.'

Platt nodded, still staring at the prosthetic leg he had set aside on the table next to the bone screws. He wrapped his hands around his coffee mug then looked up at Captain Ganz.

'After the autopsy I took a look at a tissue sample from Ronnie Towers.'

'Ronnie Towers?'

'The soldier who just died,' Platt said without criticism. 'I checked the bone paste

144

used on the prosthetic, too. There were traces of the bacteria *Clostridium sordellii*. Are you familiar with it?'

Ganz scratched at his jaw. 'Isn't that usually found in soil?'

Platt nodded. 'It can also be found in fecal matter or inside intestines.'

'That doesn't make any sense.'

'Your patients' symptoms are similar to sepsis or severe toxic shock, which can be a result of an infection caused by *Clostridium sordellii*. The only problem is, I have no idea where the bacteria came from. This is something that's usually seen in one particular type of patient.'

'And what type is that?'

'Pregnant women.'

TWENTY-NINE

Danny Delveccio tossed the last of the garbage bags into the back of the Santa Rosa Island Authority pickup. He slapped the side door to let the driver know he was finished.

'See ya tomorrow, Andy.'

'Early, dude. Gonna be some killer waves.'

'Seven?'

In reply he got a thumbs-up.

Danny walked to his car, his legs tight

145

from a day of surfing followed by the routine walk up the beach to pick up garbage. Walking in the sand had been hard to get used to, especially the burn in his calves. He remembered the first week he couldn't even hold himself up on his board. Who knew picking up other people's crap could be so physically draining.

He keyed open the trunk to his Impala. Everything he owned was back here. He didn't worry about anyone stealing the car. To a thief it'd be worthless. The tires were bald, the engine had a chronic sputter, and it needed a paint job. But it was his transportation, his home, and his lifeline.

Danny grabbed a clean towel from the stash he had just washed at the laundromat. He'd shower, stop at the vending machine, then get some sleep. Andy had heard earlier that the hurricane was already in the Gulf, and as the resident expert of such things, he assured Danny that by morning the waves would be awesome.

He closed the trunk and that's when he saw the guy standing beside him. Scared the crap out of Danny. He jumped but didn't let on.

'Sorry,' the man said. 'I didn't mean to startle you. Mr. B said you usually get off work about this time. I thought you might be hungry.'

'Mr. B? Coney Island Canteen Mr. B?'

The man held out a container that smelled like heaven: melted cheese, onions, French fries.

'Yeah, I met you there earlier today, remember? I'm a salesman and Mr. B mentioned you do odd jobs for hire around the beach.'

Danny squinted but the man's face remained partly shadowed. He supposed the guy looked familiar. How could he tell from the hundreds of faces he saw every day on the beach? But if he was a friend of Mr. B's, he had to be cool.

'I wondered if you might help me load a couple of crates into my van.'

When Danny still hesitated, the guy held out the container again.

'Cheeseburger and fries plus an Andrew Jackson? Should only take about fifteen minutes.'

Danny's mouth watered. He hadn't realized how hungry he was. It beat anything he'd get in the vending machines.

'Can I eat first?'

'Sure.'

He accepted the container and popped it open. He hadn't had a burger and fries in weeks, let alone one like this. And twenty dollars for fifteen minutes of work? Danny couldn't believe his good fortune.

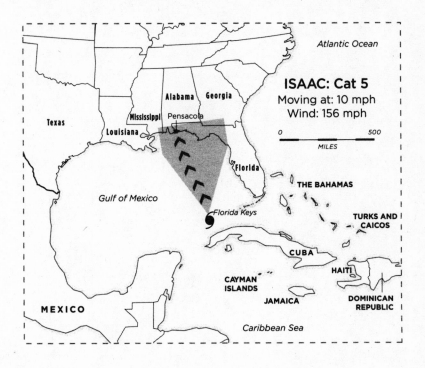

Atlantic Ocean

ISAAC: Cat 5
Moving at: 10 mph
Wind: 156 mph

0   500
MILES

Texas

Alabama   Georgia

Mississippi   Pensacola

Louisiana

Florida

Gulf of Mexico

THE BAHAMAS

Florida Keys

TURKS AND
CAICOS

CUBA

CAYMAN
ISLANDS

HAITI

JAMAICA

DOMINICAN
REPUBLIC

MEXICO

Caribbean Sea

THIRTY

Platt's vision was blurred. He tried to keep focused. If the clock on the wall was correct, it was just after one o'clock in the morning.

'I'm not a scientist, Ben,' Captain Ganz said as he rubbed his eyes, stood, and stretched behind his desk. 'You tell me this bacteria is causing an infection but you don't know where the bacteria is coming from. I can assure you these soldiers did not contract it from pregnant women.'

'No, you're missing my point.' Platt slowed himself down. They were both exhausted. He leaned against the wall, but he wanted to pace. '*Clostridium sordellii* is a rare bacterium. Most of the fatal cases that I know of have been associated with gynecologic infections following a live birth or an abortion. But I've checked. There have been other fatal cases that have nothing to do with childbirth.'

'Such as?'

Platt suppressed a yawn. He wouldn't tell Ganz that he had talked to Bix at the CDC, but he could share Bix's information. 'There was a case in Minnesota. A routine knee surgery using donated tissue.'

Ganz shook his head. 'Our donors are

151

screened and so is the tissue.'

'You screen for HIV, hepatitis B and C, and probably other blood-borne viruses. But what about bacterial diseases?'

Ganz felt behind him for his chair and dropped into it. 'Even so, only a handful of these patients have received donor tissue.'

'But all of them probably received some form of bone transplant.'

'No, that's not true.'

'The bone paste? The cement?'

'Wait a minute. Just because you found this bacteria in one patient doesn't mean it's in the others.'

Platt pulled out of his shirt pocket a crumpled piece of paper where he had jotted down a few notes from his online search. 'Does this sound familiar? Two to seven days after a surgical procedure or childbirth the patient complains of severe abdominal pain along with nausea and vomiting but no fever, no hypertension. When the symptoms finally show up, sepsis has already set in. The patient goes into toxic shock. About 70 to 80 percent of patients die within two to six days of developing the infection.'

Ganz continued to shake his head. 'Does this infection spread from person to person?'

'It's not quite known how or if it's spread from person to person or from the environment to a person. But I'll give you my best logical guess as to what might have happened in this case.'

Platt waited for the captain's attention.

'Of course. Go ahead.'

Platt sat down so they would be at eye level. He kept from crossing his arms or legs. He restrained from fidgeting and folded his hands together so he wouldn't be tapping his fingers on the table.

'Just suppose for a minute that a donor's body – for whatever reason – wasn't discovered and refrigerated or properly processed within twelve hours.'

'Eighteen hours.'

'Excuse me?'

'Eighteen hours is the time limit. Our regulations say over eighteen hours is not usable.'

'Okay, eighteen. Once the blood flow stops, you know as well as I do that decomposition starts. Depending on the conditions, it can start almost immediately. My guess is that this bacterium didn't come from contaminated tools used to process the tissue or even during surgery. I believe the bacterium came from the donor's body after death when the body started decomposing. And when that donor's tissue and bone was used to make bone screws and anchors and paste, the bacteria simply got ground up and divided. As soon as it was placed back inside a warm human body, it did what

153

bacteria loves to do – it grew and it spread by way of infection.'

Silence. Ganz stared at him. Platt realized it was a lot to sort through, but he never would have predicted what the captain said next.

'I appreciate your opinion and that you came all this way on such short notice. It's obvious that you could use some rest.'

Ganz stood again, and this time Platt stared up at him. Was it possible the captain was dismissing him? Dismissing his theory?

'I'll call my driver for you.'

And with that, Captain Ganz walked out of the room, leaving Platt dumbfounded. He wasn't just dismissing his theory, he was sending Platt home.

THIRTY-ONE

'Don't take this the wrong way, O'Dell, but you look like something the cat dragged in.'

Maggie didn't want to tell Charlie Wurth that she felt a little bit like she had been dragged. She'd been up all night with insomnia.

After her helicopter adventure she should have been exhausted enough to fall into bed and sleep. Instead, she found herself on the beach from midnight till two in the morning walking the shore and watching the full moon light up the waves. Liz had warned her that it wasn't safe to be alone on the beach at night. But Maggie figured that advice didn't apply if you carried a .38 Smith & Wesson stuffed in your waistband.

'Couldn't sleep,' she told Wurth and left it at that. No sense explaining about leaky compartments in her subconscious and ghosts from past murder cases keeping her awake at night.

Wurth had promised a real breakfast. Now, as he held open the door to the café, Maggie realized that she shouldn't have been surprised to see a number of strangers waving and saying 'good morning' and 'hello.' Less than twenty-four hours in the city and Charlie Wurth not only knew his way around but also seemed to know the hot spot for breakfast.

The Coffee Cup in downtown Pensacola was crowded, some clientele in shirts and ties with BlackBerrys and others in boots and jeans with the local newspaper scattered across the tabletop.

Despite the clatter of stoneware, the sizzle of bacon, and the shouts of waitresses to the short-order cooks, several customers immediately recognized Wurth. A businessman at a window table waved a hello and another at the counter looked up from his conversation to nod at him. A tall, skinny waitress called him 'hon' like they were old friends and led them to a table that was still being bussed. As soon as they sat, she handed them menus.

'Two coffees?' she said, plopping down stoneware mugs in front of them.

'Black coffee for me, Rita. Diet Pepsi for my partner, here.'

'Diet Coke okay, hon?' But she asked Wurth, not Maggie, while she retrieved the mug in front of her as quickly as she had set it down.

Wurth looked to Maggie and waited for an answer, which made Rita look to Maggie. She had to give him credit. It would have been so much easier to just say yes. But it was a big deal to Charlie Wurth that the people surrounding him were always acknowledged.

'Diet Coke's fine,' Maggie said.

She waited for the waitress to leave while taking in the café's surroundings. Then she leaned across the small table. 'How do you already know all these people?'

'Had coffee here yesterday. You can meet all the movers and shakers in a community if you find their watering hole.'

He paused to wave at two women who had just come in.

'And believe me,' he smiled and leaned in, 'with a hurricane coming, the federal guy who's promising to bring the cavalry is

156

much more popular than Jim Cantore from the Weather Channel. You'll see there's already a couple of signs telling him to stay the hell away.'

'Who's Jim Cantore?'

He tilted his head at her, trying to tell if she was serious. 'I forget you're a hurricane neophyte. With the last several storms, anywhere Cantore goes so goes the hurricane. He either has an uncanny ability to predict or he's a jinx. Either way, nobody wants to see him here.'

'Is he here?'

'If he isn't, he will be. It's looking like the Panhandle is Isaac's bull's-eye.'

He sat back when he saw the waitress heading to their table. She brought Maggie's Diet Coke and a pot of steaming coffee to fill Wurth's mug.

'So what can I get you two?' This time she included Maggie.

'I'll have a cheese-and-mushroom omelet.'

The waitress kept looking at her like she was waiting for more. Finally she said, 'That's it, hon?'

'You gotta have some grits with that,' Wurth told her. 'Bring her some grits, Rita. I'll have two eggs scrambled, sausage links, wheat toast, hash browns, and the Nassau grits.'

As soon as Rita turned to leave, Maggie raised her eyebrow at Wurth's breakfast order.

'What? There's a hurricane coming. Might be the last hot meal I get,' he said.

He glanced around and leaned in again.

'This one's looking bad. Bulldozed over Cuba like it was a speed bump. Land masses usually slow them down a little. Instead, Isaac's entering the Gulf as a cat 5, sustained winds at 156 miles per hour. There's nothing between here and there to slow it down. Another day over warm waters and this monster might pick up even more steam. If it makes landfall as a cat 5, that's brutal. We're no longer talking about damage, we're talking catastrophic damage.'

Maggie's eyes darted around but she stayed with elbows on the table, hands circling her condensation-drenched plastic glass. 'I guess I'm surprised there doesn't seem to be much panic or anxiety.'

'Oh, there's anxiety. Long lines yesterday. Hardware stores are sold out of generators and plywood. Grocery stores' shelves are picked clean. Can't find any bagged ice or bottled water. Most of the gas stations are pumped dry or just about there. But these folks' – Wurth pointed discreetly with his chin – 'they look out for themselves and their neighbors. They know the drill. The Panhandle has already had a couple of tropical storms hit earlier this year, and with three hurricanes making landfall on Florida, they realize their odds.

'That's the locals. Now the transplants – and there are plenty of them – they're the ones I have to convince to evacuate and get to a shelter. The city commissioners will be declaring a state of emergency later this morning. You watch. We start getting closer to the realization that this storm's gonna hit, that quiet anxiety will boil. Tempers will flare. Patience wears thin. We'll start getting some pushing and shoving.'

Rita appeared again with half a dozen plates to set on their table. Maggie had to admit, everything smelled wonderful and it reminded her that she hadn't had dinner last night.

She sliced into the omelet with her fork and melted cheese oozed out. Wurth scooped his grits into his scrambled eggs and using a slice of toast as a wedge he proceeded to wolf down the concoction.

'I haven't exactly figured out what to do with you,' he said in between bites.

'You'll drop me at the morgue. I can probably find my way back to the hotel.'

He shook his head, smothering his hash browns with salt and pepper. 'No, no, I can pick you up and get you back to the hotel. I mean during the hurricane. We won't be able to stay on the beach. Actually, most of the hotel guests were checking out this morning. The manager's doing us a favor letting us stay until he's ordered to leave. Which will probably be tomorrow, depending on how soon the outer bands hit.'

'Ordered to leave?'

'Mandatory evacuation on the beach and in low-lying areas. Sheriff's department goes door to door. Anyone wants to stay they have to sign off that they're doing so at their own risk and are relieving the authorities of any further obligation.'

'Where will you be during the storm?'

'Probably working one of the shelters.'

'Then I'll work one of the shelters.'

'I can't ask you to do that, Maggie.'

'You're not asking. I'm volunteering.'

He put his fork down and sat back to look at her. 'I don't know what I was thinking when I asked you to ride down here with me. All three hurricanes this season I've been the anti-Jim Cantore. Wherever I was sent, the storm turned and headed in the opposite direction. But I should have known my luck would change. Now I've brought you smack-dab in the middle and this one looks like it'll be a monster.'

'Charlie, I can take care of myself. It's one storm. How bad can it be?'

The look he gave her said she had no idea.

THIRTY-TWO

Scott Larsen had left before Trish woke up. He felt like he hadn't slept at all. His eyelids were heavy. His head throbbed. His mouth insisted he had swallowed a wad of cotton. Even his hair hurt when he combed it. Never again would he drink so much. In fact, he didn't care if he had an ounce of alcohol ever again.

To make matters worse, he saw Joe had been back to the funeral home. One tap of a button and the alarm system revealed that someone using Scott's key and code had entered at 3:10 in the morning and left at 4:00. What the hell was Joe doing?

Scott hoped he wouldn't be sorry he had given Joe the code. As he came in the back door of the funeral home he caught himself wincing, the throbbing in his head bouncing off the backs of his eyeballs. He dreaded finding another mess in the embalming room. He could already smell the pungent odor of cleaners mixed with ... what was that? Oh, yeah. Menthol.

He stopped before he got to the doorway. Clean. Thank God, it was clean. So the odors were from their afternoon work.

161

Maybe Joe had added some specimens to the walk-in fridge. Scott was on his way to check when the buzzer at the back door went off. He glanced at his watch. The power guy he had called earlier was right on time. Damn well should be for what they were charging just to show Scott where to flip a switch for the generator.

'Mr. Larsen?' The guy towered over Scott. Or maybe the massive tool belt and size-twelve work boots made the man seem huge. An embroidered patch on his breast pocket said his name was Ted.

'That's right, I'm Larsen,' Scott told him while he straightened his tie. It was a nervous habit and he stopped himself. Stupid to think he needed to show some authority with this guy. 'I think all the electrical stuff is outside, around back.'

Scott led the way. He could feel sweat sliding down his back and sticking to his crisply pressed shirt. Luckily he kept spares in the office. Nobody trusted a sweaty funeral director.

The sky was murky, but it didn't seem to block out the heat. If anything it heightened the humidity. Scott noticed the wind had picked up. Son of a bitch, that storm might actually hit.

'Here it is.' He pointed to the rectangular metal boxes with electrical wires weaving their way out of the top and bottom.

162

Ted flipped open the box's door.

'Yeah, you're all set up.'

Scott held back a sigh of relief. Of course, he was set up. He just needed to know how to turn the damn generator on.

'You push this button.' Ted pointed. 'Followed by this one. That sequence, okay?' He was talking to him as if Scott were a third-grader.

'Yeah, sure. No problem.' Scott answered, wanting to add 'bastard.'

'Then you pull this lever.'

'Got it. Guess I'm good to go.' He turned, ready to walk the guy back.

'Wait a minute. What's this one?' Ted had opened the other box.

'Oh that's some stuff I added when I bought the place. A walkway to connect the buildings. Brand-new walk-in cooler. Couple of freezers. The old ones were too small. Pretty outdated.'

'You know that everything on this circuit board isn't connected?'

'What are you talking about?'

'You won't have generator power for anything you added on these circuits.'

'No, that can't be right.'

'It's not connected.' Ted pointed down below both boxes.

'Will it take long for you to connect it?'

Ted laughed. Then he must have seen the panic on Scott's face. 'Sorry, man. Even if I

163

could connect it, your current generator wouldn't have enough juice for everything on the second panel.'

'What the hell am I supposed to do?'

'If you have a separate generator, you can hook it up directly. Make sure you use the double-insulated power cord. You say you've got a walk-in cooler. That's probably going to need 5500 all to itself.'

'So I just go out and buy a 5500 generator. No problem.'

'Go out and buy one? You mean you don't already have another generator?'

'No.'

'Maybe you could use your home one.'

'I don't have a home one. So I need to go to Home Depot or Lowe's and get one?'

Now the guy laughed again. 'I don't think you'll find one. Not around Pensacola anyway. My guess is they're sold out.'

THIRTY-THREE

Liz brought in the *Pensacola News Journal* and handed it to her dad on the way back to the kitchen.

'Thank you, darling.'

'Dad, you'll never guess who I ran into on the beach last night.'

164

'Who's that?'

'Scott.'

'Scott?'

'Scott Larsen, your son-in-law.'

'Scott? At the beach? Scott never goes to the beach.'

'Well, he was there last night and he was drunk.'

'Drunk? Scott? Scott doesn't drink.'

'Very drunk.'

'Maybe a beer now and then. That's about all I've ever seen him drink. What are you doing there?' He had followed her into the kitchen and was standing beside her, more interested in the stove top than in anything she was saying.

'I'm fixing us breakfast.'

'Eggs and bacon?'

'Dippy eggs.' That's what he called them because he liked to dip his toast into the yolk. When he didn't answer she added, 'Sunny-side up, right? Or have you changed your preference.'

'No, no, that's perfect.' He stayed watching. 'You can cook?'

'Dad, I've lived on my own for eight years now. What do you think I do? Eat out all the time?'

'Trish always said you didn't cook.'

'Yeah, I bet she did.'

'So what did Trish say?'

'About what?'

'About Scott being drunk.'

'I didn't tell her.'

'She wasn't with him?'

'Uh, noooo. You think he would be drunk if Trish was with him?'

'He's an odd duck. Won't even have a beer with me.'

Walter shook his head. Now at the refrigerator he poured orange juice for both of them. Then he did something that almost made Liz drop her spatula. He started setting the table: plates, coffee cups, sugar bowl, cream, silverware, even napkins and place mats. She stopped herself from commenting. Trish would have to correct him, make sure he switched the fork to the other side of the plate or that he folded the napkin. Liz just dropped bread in the toaster.

'I'm off until noon today,' she told him. 'Anything I can do to help you?'

'In the canteen?'

'No, Dad. Here at the house. For the hurricane. Did you get everything you need? I'm sure store shelves are picked over by today.'

'Apple Market had all their refrigerated items discounted. Ground beef, twenty-five cents a pound.'

'Aren't your own refrigerators full enough?'

'Maybe I'll take the grill and do up a few burgers alongside the hot dogs.'

'Are you really taking the canteen out on

166

the beach today?'

'Thought I would for a few hours around lunch.'

'People are going to be packing up. Everything will be closing down.'

'Exactly, and folks are still gonna need to get a bite to eat.'

She prepared their plates and, again, stopped herself from commenting. The canteen had saved him. Liz was willing to recognize that even if Trish wasn't. It had given him something to do after their mom was gone. He didn't need the money. The house was paid for and his pension as a retired navy commander seemed to be more than enough for him. But he did need the routine the Coney Island Canteen had brought into his life. More important, it surrounded him with people. Everybody on the beach knew the hot-dog man, or if they knew him well, it was 'Mr. B.'

'So what will they have you doing today?' he asked as he dipped the corner of his toast into his egg yolk.

'Little bit of everything, I imagine. Patrolling the waters, warning boaters, at least until the winds get out of hand. Then we'll probably be helping evacuate.'

'You know Danny? Works on the beach cleanup crew? Little guy. Loves to surf.'

She watched her dad out of the corner of her eye. He was devouring her breakfast and she wanted to smile. That was probably the biggest compliment Walter Bailey could pay her.

'I've seen him around.'

'Lives in his car. An old red Chevy Impala.'

'Yeah, he lives in that car?'

'Make sure he evacuates, would you? He's from Kansas where they try to outrun tornadoes. I just want to make sure he doesn't think he can do the same with a hurricane.'

'Sure. I'll look for him.'

'Say, whatever happened to that fishing cooler?'

Before Liz could answer there was a knock at the front door, a twist of a key followed by, 'Hello, hello.'

Trish stomped into the kitchen. She didn't seem to notice that she was interrupting a meal. She led off with: 'I'm going to kill that husband of mine.'

THIRTY-FOUR

Maggie stared down at the male torso on the stainless-steel table and couldn't help thinking how much it looked like a slab of meat.

'Body was refrigerated, possibly frozen,'

168

Dr. Tomich, the medical examiner, said into the wireless microphone clipped to the top of his scrubs. His comments were meant for his recorded notes, not necessarily for his audience. 'Cuts are precise. Efficient, but not surgical.'

'What does that mean?' the Escambia County sheriff asked from the corner. This morning he paced out his impatience along the wall of the autopsy suite. 'I don't want to be in the way,' he'd said earlier. But he didn't want to miss anything, either.

Technically the contents of the fishing cooler were under Sheriff Clayton's jurisdiction. When pieces of a body are found, the county with the heart – in this case, the whole torso – usually holds jurisdiction. Maggie had watched law enforcement agencies argue over who got to be in charge. This sheriff had put up a good fight to *not* be in charge. In his defense, Maggie understood that he was preoccupied with hurricane preparations. Making sure people were safe and ready for the storm certainly held more urgency than a body that had been missing and frozen for who knew how long.

'It means the person who did this knew how to dismember a body. But he or she is not necessarily a doctor or surgeon.'

'How can you be so sure?'

Tomich straightened from his hunched-over examination. He reminded Maggie of Spencer Tracy: silver-gray hair, black square glasses framing sparkling blue eyes that could pierce as well as charm. The Eastern European accent – Russian, maybe Polish – threw the image off a bit. When he turned to look at Clayton again, he reminded her more of her high-school history teacher, who also had been able to quiet his students with that piercing glare.

'I'm just saying' – the sheriff would not be deterred – 'where do you learn to do this to a body if not medical school?'

'Perhaps practice?' Maggie interrupted and both men furrowed their brows, almost in unison. 'Serial killers oftentimes perfect their craft simply by trial and error.'

'You're presuming who did this has done it before?' Tomich admonished.

'Can you tell me with any certainty that he has not done it before?'

This time he looked perplexed rather than irritated. 'Let me rephrase. You are presuming foul play. As of this moment I don't know the cause of death. And I do not see any evidence of murder.'

'Come on, Doc,' Clayton said. 'How do pieces of a person end up in a fishing cooler in the Gulf if it's not foul play?'

Maggie was interested in the answer but the sheriff interrupted himself.

'What's that smell?' He sniffed the air but

still didn't venture any closer to the autopsy table.

'Menthol?'

'Vicks VapoRub,' Maggie said with certainty.

'That's weird.' The sheriff was still sniffing.

'Not necessarily,' Maggie assured him. 'Not if you want to cover up the smell of decomposition.'

'Still, it indicates no evidence of foul play,' the medical examiner insisted.

A man in blue scrubs came through a side door, wheeling a stainless-steel cart. At first Maggie thought he was another doctor or pathologist until he said to Tomich, 'Here are the other contents, sir.'

'Thank you, Matthew.'

'The X-rays are on the shelf below. I'll be next door if you need me.'

'Next door? Boiling my bones?'

'Yes, sir.'

Tomich looked from Maggie to Clayton, enjoying their wide-eyed reaction.

'Someone found a set of buried bones. I doubt they're human but we shall see. Matthew is my faithful diener. He gets to have all the fun.'

'Right. All the fun.' The young man smiled as if it was a joke they shared. He certainly didn't seem to mind what sounded like a grunt assignment of boiling bones when, in

171

fact, most dieners Maggie had met in the past were as proficient at dissection as their bosses.

Matthew left and Tomich pulled down his plastic goggles. He picked up the electric bone saw, ready to cut. Maggie watched the sheriff's face lose all color.

'Oh hey, I have to make a few phone calls,' he said, pointing a thumb at the door and doing a remarkable job of keeping the panic out of his voice.

Tomich watched him leave, waited for the door to latch shut behind him. He turned back to the task at hand. Without looking at Maggie he shook his head and said, 'Politicians. I should ban them from my autopsies.' Suddenly he glanced up at her. 'You don't mind if I proceed?'

'Not at all. Please do.'

He clicked on the saw and in seconds severed the rib cage. He set the saw down. With long gloved fingers inserted in each side he opened the front of the chest, spreading the ribs and exposing the heart and lungs. Almost immediately he noticed something and started poking around inside.

'What is it?' Maggie wanted to know.

'I believe we are in luck. I shall be able to tell you exactly who our victim is.' He grabbed a forceps and a scalpel and began cutting.

THIRTY-FIVE

Scott worked his way through the Yellow Pages. How could there not be a single generator left in this city? He'd even called Mobile and Tallahassee. The last Home Depot manager he talked to had just laughed at him. Couldn't stop laughing. Scott finally hung up on the asshole.

He didn't have any employees coming in until after lunch today. He hadn't even started preparing for the memorial service. He'd make his people earn their keep today. Thank God he didn't have to embalm the body. The family had opted for a closed casket. They'd never know that dear Uncle Mel wasn't even inside. It was the storm's fault, not his. If the electricity went out and he didn't have a generator for the walk-in refrigerator, he couldn't just take all those body parts home with him.

'Oh, by the way, Trish,' he imagined saying, 'I've got a few things to stuff into our fridge.' Not like he had room there, either. He wasn't like his father-in-law with two extra refrigerators in the garage.

His father-in-law also had more than one generator. He was sure of it. He put the phone down. In fact, during the last hurricane threat Walter had bragged about having two or three generators. Why hadn't Scott thought about it sooner? He could just borrow one. No, Walter would never lend him something that substantial. Would he? No. He was fussy about his possessions. That included his daughter.

The only other alternative was to move everything from the walk-in cooler to the stand-alone freezers.

The buzzer for the back door startled him. This time it was FedEx.

The guy had already unloaded two boxes and dropped a third on top as he handed Scott the electronic signature pad.

'The tag doesn't say anything about liquids,' the guy told Scott. 'Whatever that is' – he pointed at the last box and the pink fluid oozing through the seam and running down the side – 'it's probably against regulations.'

'I'm not the one who sent it.' Scott put up his hands in defense.

The guy didn't say anything, just gave him an accusing look and headed back to his truck. Scott scooped up the boxes and moved them inside the door, out of sight and out of the heat. These had to be the deliveries Joe had mentioned. But he had gotten sloppy and not wrapped them properly. What was Joe thinking?

Scott picked up the leaking package, grabbed a towel, and wrapped it around the busted seam. He hauled the box to the walk-in cooler and decided to leave the packages for Joe to deal with. Once inside the cooler Scott stopped, almost dropping the box. On a gurney in the middle of the floor was the naked corpse of a boy. On closer inspection he realized it was a small young man.

Joe hadn't mentioned a body, only parts. Did he intend to disarticulate this one, too, before the storm hit? And exactly how and from where had he transported a corpse in the middle of a Sunday night?

Scott guessed it was possible that Joe simply picked it up from another one of his networks. He had told Scott when they first met that he obtained corpses from university donor programs, county morgues, and crematories. That's probably what happened. Some other place was unloading inventory before the storm.

Oh that was just–

This time Scott did drop the box. Either he was going nuts or that corpse just moved.

THIRTY-SIX

Maggie didn't recognize the contraption Dr. Tomich had extracted from the torso, but she had a good idea what it meant. Sheriff Clayton had returned and now he stood at the sink, his lanky frame towering over Dr. Tomich's hunched right shoulder.

'It's a defibrillator,' Dr. Tomich said as he flushed it with water, keeping the device pinched between his forceps. He reached to the side, practically elbowing Sheriff Clayton out of his way, and punched the intercom button.

'Matthew, come here. I need you to look up a serial number.'

'It seems too easy,' Clayton said. 'You're telling us there's a number on this apparatus and you'll be able to match it to a name?'

'Yes. That is exactly what I am telling you.'

'Sir.' Matthew was there in the room before anyone heard him enter.

Maggie found herself checking out his footwear, except he wore paper shoe covers like the rest of them.

Dr. Tomich placed the defibrillator onto a stainless-steel tray and handed it to Matthew.

176

'Look this up, please. Bring me the patient's name and the physician's.'

'Yes, sir.'

As the medical examiner returned to the torso, he caught Maggie eyeing the cart with the severed foot and hands.

'You're intrigued with the parts.'

It was an odd thing to say.

'Occupational hazard,' she answered, without further explanation.

Tomich nodded, bowed his head as if paying homage, then he did something Maggie didn't expect. He picked up the severed foot and placed it on a separate stainless-steel table.

'We'll take a look,' he said. He poked his glasses up the bridge of his nose with one gloved hand and waved his other at the torso. 'This gentleman won't mind if we wait for Matthew to tell us his name.'

It was an unexpected and rare courtesy. Maggie knew her surprise registered on her face, but Dr. Tomich didn't notice. He was already pulling open a new tray of instruments and resetting his wireless recording. Sheriff Clayton, who had been squeamish about watching the torso, didn't have a problem with getting a closer look at the severed foot.

'Are you trying to match any of these to one of your cases?'

It took Maggie a second to realize that

Tomich was talking to her and not his wireless.

'Not this time. How many different victims do you think are here?'

'At least two.' Tomich slouched over the table as he began his examination. 'Or it could be five. I may be able to tell you that quickly with a simple blood test. Process of elimination. If all the parts are the same blood type, we'll need to wait for DNA tests.'

'If the hands don't belong to the torso,' Sheriff Clayton asked, 'we might not figure out whose they are. Fingerprints don't make much difference if we can't match them to somebody already in the system.'

'This is interesting.' Dr. Tomich poked at the ankle. 'Something beneath the skin.'

He picked up the scalpel and moved the severed foot onto its side, the inside of the ankle facing up. At first glimpse the object Dr. Tomich began to remove looked like a piece of metal. Another medical device? A pin or clip jabbing its way up to the surface?

Tomich cut, then held the small object up to the light, clasped in his forceps.

'Is it a bullet fragment?' Sheriff Clayton asked.

The medical examiner gave it only a cursory look before dropping it into a stainless-steel basin.

'There's more,' Tomich said.

One after another he plucked and

dropped into the basin four more pieces of metal that had been embedded deep into the foot.

'Shotgun?' asked the sheriff.

Before the medical examiner had a chance to decide, Matthew appeared alongside of them. This time the sheriff jumped, but cleared his throat and shifted his weight as if he had been just readjusting his stance.

'Sir, I have the information you requested.'

'The patient who belongs to the defibrillator? This soon?'

'Yes, sir. The number is registered to Vince Coffland of Port St. Lucie, Florida.'

'Port St. Lucie?' Sheriff Clayton interrupted. 'That's over six hundred miles away. And it's on the Atlantic side. How the hell did he end up in a cooler floating in the Gulf?'

'Any information on what happened to Mr. Coffland?' Tomich asked his diener.

'He's been missing since July tenth. He disappeared after Hurricane Gaston.'

'Missing?'

'Disappeared.'

THIRTY-SEVEN

Sometimes a corpse moved. Scott knew it was a fact that no one liked to talk about except at conferences after a few drinks. It'd never happened to Scott, but he'd heard stories of others who had experienced what they called 'spontaneous movement.' A leg or a foot twitched. He couldn't remember exactly what caused it. Some kind of bio-chemical reaction. But it usually occurred in the first ten to twelve hours after death. Maybe that's all this was, but when Scott called Joe he opted for the extreme. After the morning he'd experienced, he couldn't hide the stress.

'That stiff you left in my cooler is still alive.'

'What are you talking about?'

'He moved.'

Silence. Long enough that Scott second-guessed his approach. Would Joe think his partner prone to hysterics? That he couldn't handle the extra business?

'Look, man,' Joe finally said in his usual calm and cool manner, 'it's just your im-agination playing tricks on you.' Then he added like a buddy, a friend, 'Dude, you did have a lot to drink last night.'

There was something about Joe's voice – his calling him 'dude' – that made Scott relax ... a little.

By the time Joe arrived half an hour later, Scott had almost convinced himself that it probably was just his imagination. His head still throbbed. Earlier his vision seemed blurred. He hadn't gone back into the cooler and now he felt a bit ridiculous.

Scott tried to concentrate while he kept his employees busy in the funeral home preparing the memorial service for Uncle Mel, the reclusive bachelor whose family wanted him buried before the hurricane rolled in. Scott told the employees they couldn't go to the back offices because he was fumigating the walkway. It seemed like an absurd excuse even to him. Why fumigate anything before a hurricane? But no one questioned him, which further validated his salesmanship. Damn, he was good. Even in a crisis with all the stress he could make up stuff to believable levels.

He had left Joe for twenty minutes, tops. As soon as Scott could, he sneaked back, going outside and avoiding the walkway. Joe was closing and latching the walk-in refrigerator.

'Hey Scott,' Joe said. 'I have to tell you, man, I wish you could have heard your voice. "The stiff moved."' He laughed as he slapped Scott between the shoulder blades.

'Yeah, probably too much Scotch.'

'Or not enough,' Joe said as he pulled out his money clip and started peeling off hundred-dollar bills. 'I'll have a few more specimens to add before the storm, if that's okay,' he said as he placed the bills on the corner desk.

Scott couldn't count and listen at the same time.

'I'll come back tonight. Try and cut and package up as much as possible. Take less room that way.'

'Sure, no problem.' Scott found himself saying the words while he struggled to keep his eyes away from the pile of hundred-dollar bills.

'I'd offer to take you to dinner again, but I think you might need to rest,' Joe said with a grin, the kind that went along with terms like 'dude.' 'I'll see you later.'

Scott offered a smile and a nod, feeling better as he reminded himself that this was a good business arrangement and that he really liked Joe Black. He let out a sigh. But as he watched Joe leave, Scott noticed something on the side of Joe's khaki pants. He started to point it out then stopped himself. It looked like blood. Bright red, not pink. Splattered red blood. Corpses didn't splatter blood.

THIRTY-EIGHT

This would have been a day off for Liz Bailey if it wasn't for Isaac churning a path directly at the Florida Panhandle. New projections had the storm making landfall sooner than what was earlier predicted. The wind and waves suggested the new projections were accurate.

Liz was accustomed to being out in winds like this. She wondered just how used to it Lieutenant Commander Wilson was. He tight-fisted the controls and fought against each gust. It felt like being in a car with the driver constantly accelerating, braking, and accelerating again, combined with an occasional roller-coaster plunge.

Kesnick looked at her. With his back safely to Wilson and Ellis, he rolled his eyes. She held back a smile.

From above they watched boaters coming in early, heeding the weather advisories. All the marinas were full, with lines of crafts waiting to tie up. There was no surefire protection outside of pulling your boat out of the water and hauling it as far north as possible. Some people were trying to do that by motoring up rivers and paying to dock their boats in places out of the storm's path.

They were seeing an early surge. Waves already pounded seawalls and crashed up the beach, reaching the sand dunes. Surfers dotted in between the waves, bright spots of color bobbing up and down, disappearing and springing back into sight.

In the helicopter, Liz kept reminding herself to take it all in and remember how everything looked before Isaac hit. In 2004 Hurricane Ivan had decimated the area, ripping apart and chewing up everything in its path. The Florida Panhandle was where pine trees met palm trees, and the national forests that covered acres of land became shredded sticks, many snapped in two. Four-lane highways looked like a monster had taken a bite out of the asphalt, chewed it up, and spit it out. The massive live oaks, hundreds of years old, that lined Santa Rosa Sound were blown over, their tangled roots two stories high.

Pensacola Beach is about eight miles long and only a quarter mile at its widest, a peninsula with Santa Rosa Sound on one side and the Gulf of Mexico on the other. During Ivan the two bodies of water looked like one, meeting in the middle.

Liz remembered that it had taken years to sift and separate the debris from the sand. Huge machines had occupied the coastline. Cranes became a part of the skyline. Bluetarped rooftops were seen in every neighborhood. Hurricanes never discriminated.

The three-mile I-10 bridge between Escambia County and Santa Rosa County had taken three years to repair. It had been crippling for a community connected by bridges to have all four major ones compromised in some way by the storm's massive surge.

Liz hadn't been here for Ivan, only for the aftermath. She had just finished training in Elizabeth City, North Carolina. For some reason she always regretted missing the actual storm. Silly. Not like she could have made a difference. It was probably some form of survivor's guilt. Perhaps she would be able to make a difference this time.

THIRTY-NINE

Walter Bailey decided to close up for the day despite the steady stream of customers. He didn't like the way the wind had started to rock the canteen back and forth. He'd bought the mobile unit at the navy commissary three years ago, not looking for a business but rather for something to do. He and his wife, Emilie, had looked forward to his early retirement. After all those years of six-month cruises and being apart, the two of

185

them had a long list of plans, things they'd never been able to do between assignments. Emilie died before they'd even gotten started.

Within the first year of her absence, Walter realized that all his new hobbies seemed to be things other people called addictions. He had to come to terms with the simple fact that nothing would stop the ache. There were certain losses, certain voids that could never be filled with anything other than that which left the void in the first place.

These days he just wanted to stay busy. That's where the Coney Island Canteen came in. The mobile canteen had been in sad shape when Walter bought it, weathered and rusted but still in good working condition. He'd scraped and cleaned and polished the stainless-steel inside, painted the outside red, white, and blue, hung curtains with stars and stripes, and named it after one of his favorite boyhood places. It had never been about making money. Instead, it was something to occupy his time and keep him company so he wouldn't think about the void, about that empty hole that was left in his heart.

'You packing up, Walter?'

He poked his head out the side door to find Charlotte Mills in her signature floppy hat and cat-eye sunglasses, the hat too big and the glasses too bright for her small, meek features. Her pants legs were rolled up

186

and she wore a long-tailed white cotton shirt over a formfitting tank top. Yellow flip-flops accentuated bright-red toenails. Her pockets bulged with seashells. Before he had gotten to know her, he'd called her the beachcombing widow – but only in his mind.

'I have a couple of dogs still warm if you're interested.'

'Only if you have time. Everyone seems in a hurry today.'

'Aren't you packing up?'

'Humph.' She waved a birdlike hand at him. 'I've gone through worse than what's coming. Last time I left, they wouldn't let us back on the beach for weeks.'

'If I remember correctly, the bridge was out.'

'Or so they said.'

Years ago Charlotte's husband was killed in a plane crash, just days before he was to testify in a federal investigation against a state senator. There was never any evidence that the crash had been anything more than an unfortunate accident, but Charlotte believed otherwise. Walter wondered if she had always been prone to conspiracy theories because she saw them everywhere now.

'This storm's gonna be bad.' Walter had slid the window back open and started pulling out condiments to prepare her hot dog. He decided to fix himself one and join her. 'If you need a place to stay, you're welcome to come to my house. I'm well above the floodplain and about a quarter mile from Escambia Bay. It'll just be me, my daughter, and maybe my son-in-law.'

'That's so sweet, Walter. But no, I'm staying. Already got the plywood up. Plenty of batteries and the generator's ready to go in the garage.'

'Now, Charlotte, remember how Ivan shoved water and sand right through most of these beach houses?'

'Mine's cinder block. It made it through Ivan, I'm sure it'll make it through this.'

'Hey, Mr. B.'

'Well, if it isn't Phillip Norris's son.'

Walter almost regretted remembering the name of the young man's father. The look on Norris's face was a combination of shock and embarrassment. It was obvious he hadn't wanted Walter to remember.

He introduced Charlotte, giving the young man the opportunity to introduce himself only if he chose to. Walter was pleased, but surprised, when Norris held out his hand and told her, 'I'm Joe Black.'

'I was just trying to convince Charlotte that she needed to leave the beach during the storm.'

'I have a nice, solid, two-story cinder-block house, one lot back from the water. I'll be fine.'

'People disappear during hurricanes,' Joe

said, and both Walter and Charlotte stared at him, startled at his bluntness. 'There were more than three hundred people who went missing after Hurricane Ike hit Galveston, Texas. I'm just saying it happens. You really might want to reconsider.'

FORTY

Maggie spent the rest of the afternoon back in her hotel room. Outside, the parking lots were filled with people packing up their belongings and getting ready to evacuate the beach. Most of the businesses were closed, the owners starting to board up windows and doors. However, surfers were still riding the waves. Some of the restaurants remained open. The Tiki Bar had a huge sign out front offering free drinks till they ran out.

The hotel manager had told Maggie he'd stay until the authorities closed the bridge. Maggie and Wurth were welcome to stay until then. Almost all of the other guests had checked out. Maggie suspected, from the absolute quiet, that she was the only one on her entire floor.

Sheriff Clayton had been gracious enough to drive her back to Pensacola Beach after the autopsy.

189

'Sorry, I can't be of much help,' the sheriff had told her. 'I'll contact Vince Coffland's next of kin. But anything else will have to wait until after the storm.'

Maggie asked him to give her cell-phone number to Coffland's widow. If she wanted to talk about the details of her husband's disappearance, Maggie would be interested in listening. Clayton agreed.

Now, as she sipped a Diet Pepsi and waited for her laptop to boot up, she kept glancing at her cell phone. No calls. No messages ... from anyone. She had the TV turned on to the Weather Channel but muted. Every once in a while she glanced at the on-screen graphics of Isaac's progression. She noticed one of the weather reporters, handsome, shaved head, nice legs, standing in front of the Gulf with its emerald-green rolling waves. She read the crawl: JIM CANTORE REPORTING FROM PENSACOLA.

'Oh Charlie, he's here.' She smiled as she started jotting down things she wanted to remember.

Clayton had been correct about the severed hands and the fingerprints. None on file. They would need to wait for DNA to see if any of the hands belonged to Vince Coffland. A simple blood test had already found the foot to be someone else's. Vince Coffland was type B. The foot's blood was type O.

On the hotel notepad she wrote:

Coffland disappeared July 10
Port St. Lucie over 600 miles
 (land miles) away
Foot: metal debris; belonged to a 2nd victim
Plastic: heavy ply (commercial use?)
Fishing cooler: Why?
Tie-down: man-made synthetic rope,
 blue and yellow fibers

Had the foot belonged to Vince Coffland, Maggie was ready with an explanation. She'd heard of storm victims – victims exposed out in the open – sometimes ending up with an odd assortment of items like pieces of insulation, asbestos, vinyl siding, and glass embedded in their skin.

She'd asked Dr. Tomich if she could borrow one of the pieces of metal. Now she fingered it, still encased inside its plastic bag. She set it on the desktop in front of her. It was definitely metal, bent and distorted. But where did it come from?

Perhaps the metal was something that had gotten ripped apart during the hurricane-force winds. If the foot didn't belong to Coffland, was it possible it belonged to another person who had gone missing during Hurricane Gaston?

She added to her list:

Maggie had handed over to Sheriff Clayton the label – or what she suspected was a label – that she found inside the cooler. However, she had memorized the faded printing and written it down exactly as it had appeared. She pulled out her copy and laid it on the desk beside the metal fragment.

AMET
DESTIN: 082409
#8509000029

She believed the second line was 'destination' and a date, 082409, which translated to August 24, 2009. She had no idea what AMET was. Probably an acronym but for what? The last line might be a serial number. It didn't, however, match the defibrillator.

Maggie glanced at the television and the map that Jim Cantore was showing of the Florida Panhandle. Then she did a double take. Off to the right side of Pensacola was Destin, Florida. Was it possible the second line of the label wasn't meant to be an abbreviation for destination, but rather Destin, Florida?

She twisted the hotel phone so she could see the instructions on its face as well as the hotel's phone number. Sure enough, 850 was the area code. The third line wasn't a serial number but a phone number.

What would it hurt to try? She tapped the number into her smartphone, pressed Call, and waited. It was ringing on the other end. Her mind kicked over to interrogation mode. She slowed her breathing, wiped her sweaty palm, and transferred the phone to her other hand. Three rings. Was the person on the other end expecting one of the packages from the cooler?

A woman's voice answered. 'Advanced Medical Educational Technology, how may I direct your call?'

Maggie's eyes darted to the piece of paper. AMET.

'Yes, I'd like to speak with someone about a delivery.'

'You have a delivery for us? Is it for one of our conferences?'

'Yes, I believe so.'

'That would be Lawrence Piper. He's off-site today. Can I have him return your call?'

Maggie gave the woman her name and phone number. Before she could hang up, her phone was already beeping with an incoming call.

'This is Maggie O'Dell.'

'Hey, it's Tully. I think I finally found your rope.'

'What is it?'

'High-tenacity rope, UV resistant, antichemical erosion, modified resin coating.'

'Wait a minute. You're able to tell all that from my photos?'

'The weave is unique. I scanned in a couple of your close-ups and got a hit.'

Maggie had hoped the rope would lead them to the killer.

'So you found the manufacturer?'

'Ningbosa Material Company. They specialize in bullet-proof plate, cut-resistant fabric, all kinds of good stuff.'

'Are they somewhere close by?'

'Zhejiang, China.'

'You're kidding.'

'I'm not sure I pronounced that correctly. My Chinese needs work.'

'I guess I shouldn't be surprised. Everything's made in China these days, right?'

'There's more. This color combination is a special order.'

'Excellent. So who's the customer?'

'The United States Navy.'

Before Maggie could respond, her phone was beeping again. Could it be Lawrence Piper already returning her call?

'I've got another call coming in,' she told Tully.

'Let me know if you need anything else.'

'Thanks.' She clicked over. 'Maggie O'Dell.'

'Now that's music to my ears.'

'Colonel Benjamin Platt.' She tried to keep

the smile from her voice. She hadn't talked to him for several days and whether she wanted to admit it to him or to herself, she missed him. 'How goes your secret mission?'

'I'm being sent home. Can I buy you dinner tomorrow night?'

'I'm not home and I won't be for several days.'

'Oh.' He sounded disappointed. Disappointed and tired.

'Long story. I ended up on a road trip to Pensacola, Florida, with Charlie Wurth. Now I'm stuck here because of the hurricane.'

'You're kidding? Where are you right now?'

'The Hilton on the beach. I'm looking out at the emerald-green waters of the Gulf as we speak. It's absolutely beautiful. Hard to imagine a hurricane is on its way.'

'Go out on your balcony.'

'Excuse me?'

'What floor are you on?'

'Platt, I swear if you ask me what I'm wearing, I'm hanging up.'

'Just go out on your balcony.'

Maggie hesitated. The balcony door was open. She had wanted to listen to the sound of the waves. She walked out onto the small balcony.

'Now look down on the beach,' Platt told her.

There he was waving up at her.

'Buy you a drink at the Tiki Bar,' he said.

FORTY-ONE

'Did I tell you how good it is to see you?' Platt asked Maggie.

'Three times.'

But she smiled when she said it, so he figured he must not sound as high-school annoying as he thought he did. She wore a yellow knit top that brought out the gold flecks in her brown eyes. And she was wearing shorts – real shorts, not the baggy athletic ones she wore on game day. And flip-flops. She never wore open-toed shoes. The whole package was distracting as hell.

They'd snagged a table looking out at the Gulf. Platt had been told that most of the tourists had left Pensacola Beach, but the restaurants and bars – the ones that were still open – were crowded with residents, tired from packing all day.

The Tiki Bar offered free drinks. Their waitress told them they could still order appetizers if they didn't mind an assortment chosen by the cook. In other words, whatever was left. When she delivered the platter, Maggie and Platt looked at each other like they had hit the jackpot: wild-mushroom spring rolls, grilled prawns with salsa, pine-

196

apple-glazed pork ribs. His mouth started watering from the aromas alone.

'You still can't tell me about your secret mission, can you?' Maggie asked him after devouring a spring roll.

'Probably not. It doesn't matter.' He wiped the glaze from his chin, sat back, and sipped a mai tai. It was his second and the rum had begun to relax him, except that he couldn't shake Ganz's abrupt shift in attitude. His finger tapped at the yellow paper umbrella and bobbed the slice of lime poked at the end. 'I gave them my opinion. They didn't like it and they sent me home.'

'Hmmm.' Maggie picked up one of the prawns. 'Sounds like a government assignment. Was it one of the military bases here?'

'How do you do that?' he said before he realized that he had just admitted she was correct.

'Look, you really don't need to tell me. I'm okay with that.'

'What about your case?'

'Coast Guard found a fishing cooler in the Gulf.'

'With a body inside?'

She nodded with a mouthful. They were across the table from each other but close enough that Platt reached over and dabbed at the corner of her mouth with a napkin.

'Sorry,' she said, grabbing her own napkin and wiping both corners now. He immedi-

197

ately regretted what had been an instinctive gesture. 'Pieces of at least one victim. A man who disappeared after Hurricane Gaston.'

'Gaston? I thought that one hit on the Atlantic side.'

'It did.'

'You think you might have a killer who preys on hurricane victims?'

'I don't know. It's possible. People go missing.'

'There is a lot of chaos and now you're stuck here to experience it.'

She shrugged. 'You must know by now that you are, too.'

'I was offered a ride to Jacksonville on a C-130.'

'A military cargo plane? Wow. How generous of them.'

Platt's turn to shrug. He still felt the sting of Ganz's dismissal.

'So just out of curiosity, what were the pieces?' he asked.

'A torso, one foot, three hands. Aren't you hungry? Because I'm about to consume all of this.'

He smiled and plucked up a spring roll. He was hungry but almost too exhausted to eat. He couldn't remember when he slept last.

'Three hands? So at least two victims.'

'It could be two people or as many as five. Blood typing has already ruled out the foot belonging to the torso.'

'So the killer's either messy or very smart. Do you think he was disposing bodies at sea?'

He could tell she was considering it then shook her head.

'The body parts were wrapped individually in thick plastic wrap, almost as if he was preserving instead of disposing.' She drained her second Diet Pepsi. 'What's worse is that the foot has pieces of metal embedded under the skin, deep into the tissue.'

'Why did Kunze send you on this wild-goose chase? And into the eye of a hurricane?'

'Long story.' She waved at the passing waitress and politely pointed to her glass for a refill. 'Where are you staying?'

'My duffel bag is at the Santa Rosa Island Authority office. They told me there were no check-ins on the beach. No rooms available anywhere else.'

'I have a suite at the Hilton. At least until tomorrow.'

'Hmmm.' He couldn't tell whether it was an invitation. They joked with each other so often that sometimes he wasn't sure where he really stood with Maggie O'Dell.

'Two queen-size beds.'

Ah, okay. An offer from his friend. Was that relief he was feeling in his gut? Or was it disappointment?

'Minibar?' he sparred back.

'Yep.'

'Big-screen TV?'

'It's a hotel room, Platt, not a sports bar.'

'You sure you don't mind sharing? I think I snore when I'm overtired.'

'Not a problem. I haven't been sleeping anyway.'

'What do you mean you haven't been sleeping? Like at all?'

She looked as though she had revealed too much. 'Bad case of insomnia,' she said.

'For how long?' The doctor in him couldn't help it. Maybe that was the reason for their inability to move past friendship. They had begun as doctor and patient when Maggie was quarantined under his directive at USAMRIID.

'I sleep a few hours now and then.' She hesitated then admitted, 'It's probably been a few months.'

'Well, I have just what you need.'

'Look, Ben, I'm not sure I want to get used to taking any meds.'

'I'm not talking about meds.' He raised his hands as if to show her. 'My massages can work wonders.'

FORTY-TWO

Scott drove past his father-in-law's house twice. Not an easy task because he lived on the edge of a cul-de-sac. He hadn't been able to get him on the phone. Walter Bailey was the only person Scott knew who didn't own a cell phone and was proud of the fact.

The front windows remained dark, not even a reflection from the TV. Walter's car was in the driveway but not his mobile canteen. Was it possible he was still out on the beach?

Scott slapped his hands against the steering wheel. That was great, just great. He needed a generator and the old man was out partying on the beach.

He had driven to five different hardware stores with a roll of cash, thinking he could surely buy a backroom generator from someone. After all, everyone had a price, didn't they?

He ignored the homemade signs in the parking lots: NO MORE PLYWOOD, GENERATORS, OR BATTERIES. At each store, he asked for the manager. Two of them just shook their heads at him. Two others laughed. One eyed the roll of cash

201

and considered selling Scott his personal home generator, then finally said, 'Hell, I better not. My wife would kick the royal crap out of me. Sorry, mister.'

'Can you at least tell me,' he asked that manager, while peeling a hundred-dollar bill off his roll, 'how far I have to drive to go get one?'

The guy started checking his computer, anxious to help if it meant a finder's fee. He poked at the keys, winced, then poked some more. He did this several times before he finally said, 'Here we go. There's one I can hold for you at the Athens, Georgia, store.'

'Athens? Okay. Is that just over the Florida/Georgia border?'

'No, it's on the north side of Atlanta.'

'Atlanta? Isn't that like five or six hours away?'

'You could be there when the store opens at seven tomorrow. You want me to put a hold on it or not?'

He told him to go ahead. It was a backup plan that only cost him a hundred bucks if he didn't need it. The more he thought about driving twelve hours, the more angry he got with his in-laws.

The Baileys had never embraced him like they should have. And he took good care of Trish. By the holidays, she'd be living in a brand-new custom-built home overlooking Pensacola Bay. He had her driving a BMW –

a fucking 525i. He made it so she didn't have to work a single day after they got married. Even the place they were renting was plush and loaded with luxury. He was acknowledged around town as a successful businessman, invited to join the Rotary. And yet all that wasn't good enough. The Baileys still didn't treat him like he was family. What was worse, Scott felt like Walter Bailey treated him as if he wasn't worthy of Trish. Walter certainly wouldn't think he was worthy of borrowing one of his fucking generators.

Scott shut off the headlights and pulled his Lexus GX to a stop along the curb half a block from Walter's house, where he could see anyone turning into the driveway. It was late. Where the hell was the old man? He drank the lukewarm remains of his latte. He had added a splash of vodka – from the previous funeral home owner's stash that he had taken along for the ride – thinking he'd need the extra jolt to convince Walter. But even that was wearing off.

He knew there was a fifty-fifty chance the side door to the garage would be unlocked – habit more than anything else. Walter couldn't park a single vehicle in the garage since it was packed with his discounts, bargains, and supplies for the canteen.

Scott scrubbed the exhaustion from his face. It had been a hell of a day. He just wanted to go home and fall into bed. But even that promised to be a challenge. Trish had left several angry voice and text messages for him.

Scott looked at his wristwatch and let out a sigh of frustration. He sure as hell was not driving to Atlanta tonight. He turned the key but left the headlights off. As quietly as the vehicle allowed, he pulled up and backed into Walter's driveway. The garage was attached to the back of the house. Even with the sliding door open no one could see into the garage from the street. If the neighbors recognized his vehicle, that would actually be a good thing. They wouldn't call the cops on Trish's husband.

The side door was unlocked. Scott used a flashlight to hunt down the generators, not really sure what they looked like. A big engine on wheels was his best guess. Two refrigerators hummed, side by side. Loaded shelves lined three of the walls. The only path amounted to a maze winding its way through boxes and cartons, toolboxes and garden equipment, spare tires, bags of mulch, large red gas containers, two push mowers – and that was just one side of the double garage.

In the corner he found a generator covered with a gray tarp. He rocked it out of a tight squeeze between two shelves. Once he pulled it free, he was ready to open the garage door. He hit the electronic button and the whine startled him as did the bright light that flashed on as the door went up. He lunged for the light switch and flipped it off. The noise was bad enough. He didn't need a spotlight on what he was doing. He dragged over the metal railings Walter had stored with the generator, figuring out that if he positioned them against the rear bumper of his Lexus he could simply roll the contraption up into the vehicle. He had it almost in when he saw the shadow walk out from behind the bushes.

'What the hell are you doing, Scott?'

FORTY-THREE

Liz couldn't believe her dad would loan Scott a generator. He was fussy about his possessions and he didn't seem to like Scott much. But what did she know about her father? She'd been surprised to find him downing free martinis, one after another, at the Tiki Bar on the beach. Liz reminded herself that a lot had changed since her mom had died, and she hadn't been here for most of that time. If her dad had learned to set the table and drink martinis, perhaps he'd changed in other ways, too.

'Hey, Liz.' Scott was out of breath but didn't seem embarrassed, and he didn't stop what he was doing. 'Do you have any idea where your dad is?'

'I just brought him and the canteen home. Free drinks on the beach.'

'Is he okay?'

'Sleeping like a baby. I have half a mind to leave him in the canteen for the night. So what are you doing?'

'Just picking up one of Walter's generators.' He slammed shut the rear door of the SUV. 'I've been waiting for him the past couple of hours.'

'He probably forgot.'

In the shadows Liz couldn't see Scott's face. After last night's run-in on the beach, she realized that she didn't know her brother-in-law very well, either, despite the fact that he thought he knew her. It looked like Trish had finally gotten him to prepare for the storm.

'You know how to hook up and start one of those?' she asked him.

Scott shrugged. 'Not really. I was hoping Walter would show me.'

Instinctively Liz looked over her shoulder. She couldn't see the canteen where she'd parked it on the street.

'Tell you what,' she told Scott, 'you help me get my dad into bed, I'll help you with the generator.'

'Really? You'd do that?' He sounded like a little boy, suspicious that he might be tricked.

'Sure. If you throw in a ride back to the beach to get my car.'

Walter proved more cooperative than Liz expected. He seemed to think Scott was an old navy friend of his. He kept mumbling something about Phillip Norris's kid. But once they got him inside his bedroom, he clicked into his routine. He mumbled and shuffled as he took off his shoes and put them where they belonged in the closet. Then he emptied his pockets into the valet tray on his dresser. Liz kissed him goodbye on the cheek and he waved her out of his bedroom.

At the funeral home Scott rolled the generator out the back of the SUV like a pro. Liz helped him fill it with gasoline. He talked too much, either because he was tired or because he was uncomfortable being alone with her. Or – and she hated that she jumped to this conclusion – because he'd been drinking. It didn't matter. She just wanted to finish here, get her car, and catch some sleep. The storm's outer bands were predicted to kick up winds and the downpour would start sometime tomorrow afternoon.

She showed Scott all the basics – how to choke the generator and how to calculate the wattage of each appliance he connected. All the while he rambled on about the new air-conditioned walkway he'd installed between the two buildings and his huge walk-in refrigerator.

'I added all this stuff only to find out none of it is connected to a backup generator. Can you imagine not having a backup for the cooler? In a funeral home?'

Finished with the instructions, she helped him pull the machine into an outdoor supply shed. It was only ten feet away from the building, hidden behind some trees.

She waited in the doorway as he spread a tarp over the generator and used bungee cords to fasten it. That's when she noticed the battered white stainless-steel cooler. It was huge. The lid had been left open, leaning up against the wall, and Liz noticed the fish-measuring ruler molded into the lid. A tie-down hung from the cooler's handle, a rope made of yellow-and-blue strands.

Liz felt a little sick to her stomach. This cooler looked exactly like the one she had pulled out of the Gulf.

FORTY-FOUR

'Oh my God, that feels good,' Maggie told Platt as he settled beside her on the edge of the bed.

'You're going to have to stop talking about this case so you can relax and enjoy this.'

What Maggie couldn't tell Platt was that

she had to keep talking because as soon as she thought about his hands on her bare back she felt herself getting aroused.

'There's an area right around here,' he said as his hands slid to her lower back. 'This should put you to sleep.'

She closed her eyes. He didn't have a clue. Or if he did, he was better at hiding it than she was.

'You didn't answer my question,' she said and wondered if she sounded just as breathless as she felt. He was right. It was starting to be difficult to concentrate but not because she was falling asleep.

'Why wrap the body parts?' Platt's hands continued without interruption. 'Maybe he's adding to a collection.'

'This fishing cooler is huge.' His fingers kneaded her skin, a combination of pressure and caress. 'Where do you buy something like that?'

'Sporting goods store? Or a place that sells boats?'

'A boat. I didn't even think of that. He must own a boat.'

'This is probably why you can't sleep,' Platt said. 'You won't let your mind shut off. You're still trying to figure things out.'

'The subconscious does continue to work through problems and then find–' His thumbs pressed into the middle of her back and took her breath away.

'That's better,' Platt said.

'So you're purposely ... trying ... to shut me up.'

'Exactly. Just for a few minutes, okay?'

'You talk then.'

'Really? You don't like silence?'

She nodded or tried to.

'Okay. If it's going to help relax you.'

He started telling her about a place where his family spent vacations when he was a boy. A cottage on the North Carolina shore. The kitchen overlooked the beach. Bright-yellow curtains and a tablecloth to match. He'd stay inside on the afternoons that his mother baked. She'd tell him to go play in the sand but he wanted to be there when the cinnamon rolls or peanut-butter cookies drizzled with sugar came out of the oven. So she'd let him help. He measured and stirred while they talked about the books he'd brought to read during vacation. They'd discuss the powers of wizards, the discovery of the *Titanic,* and whether sea dragons really existed.

At some point Maggie heard the sound of waves. She smelled the salt water, and for a second she thought she could even smell cinnamon. She had a light-headed sensation of floating on water. In her mind she saw the waves rolling, capped by white foam. Felt the spray on her face. There was nothing but water all around her. No land in sight. Just the gentle rocking of the water.

FORTY-FIVE

Liz sat in her car on the beach. Scott had dropped her off almost half an hour ago. She needed to drive home, take a shower, get some sleep. Tomorrow would be a long, hard day. And yet here she sat, staring out at the waves, her mind still reeling. Before leaving Scott, she had asked about the marine cooler, keeping her voice light and casual.

'A friend left it here. Just for a day or two,' he told her.

'A friend in the business?'

'Yeah, why?'

'No reason. I just...' She had found herself stumbling because she could still see the plastic-wrapped body parts. 'I've never seen one with a measure molded inside the lid like that.'

'Oh yeah. I didn't notice that.' He had walked around to the front of the cooler to get a better look. 'I bet Joe didn't notice it, either. He doesn't exactly use it for fishing.'

'Really? What does he use it for?'

That was where she crossed the line. She saw him shut down, a hint of suspicion replacing his need to charm and inform. In the end he shrugged like it was no big deal.

'I don't know. Whatever you use a cooler like that for.'

Then he walked her out of the shed.

Liz had already called Sheriff Joshua Clayton only to have one of his deputies call her back, saying this wasn't of an urgent nature.

'We've got a hurricane on its way,' the deputy told her. 'Sheriff Clayton has already determined this case is on hold until after the storm.'

He was right. Finding a fishing cooler that looked like the one filled with body parts didn't seem urgent. But something about finding it in the back of a funeral home kept Liz from dismissing it.

She could see the top floor of the Hilton. She pulled out her cell phone again. Punched 411 and asked for the phone number.

'Hilton Pensacola Beach Gulf Front. This is the front desk.'

'Yes, I'd like to talk to one of your guests. Maggie O'Dell.'

'All of our guests have checked out. Oh, wait. O'Dell. The FBI agent with Mr. Wurth?'

'Yes, that's right.'

'She is here until noon tomorrow.' Then he hesitated. 'Is this urgent?'

Liz sighed, ran fingers through her hair as she checked the time on her dashboard. It was almost midnight.

'It's just that I usually don't ring my guests' rooms after ten o'clock,' he said when she took too long to answer. 'I can send you to voice mail and the red light will come on her phone.'

'That's fine.'

While she waited for the connection, she tried to formulate what to say. Was she simply being paranoid? Overly observant? Obsessive?

At the beep she gave her name and cell-phone number, then simply said she had some information. Lame, she knew, but safe. And maybe in the morning when the outer bands of Hurricane Isaac started battering the area, Liz would think the identical fishing cooler was nothing but a mere coincidence.

There were only a few cars left in the lot and as Liz pulled onto Pensacola Beach Boulevard she recognized the faded red Impala. She had promised her dad she'd check on the surfer kid, Danny. She'd talk to him tomorrow. It was late. No sense in tapping on his car window tonight and scaring the poor kid to death.

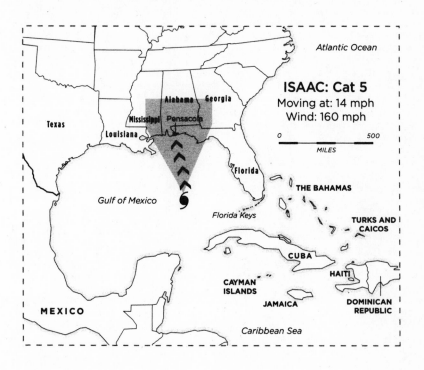

Atlantic Ocean

ISAAC: Cat 5
Moving at: 14 mph
Wind: 160 mph

0   500

MILES

Texas

Alabama   Georgia

Mississippi   Pensacola

Louisiana

Florida

Gulf of Mexico

THE BAHAMAS

Florida Keys

**TURKS AND
CAICOS**

CUBA

**CAYMAN
ISLANDS**

HAITI

JAMAICA

**DOMINICAN
REPUBLIC**

MEXICO

Caribbean Sea

FORTY-SIX

The pounding came from someplace other than inside Platt's head. Of that he was certain, though the back of his head throbbed. He opened his eyes and took a few seconds to remember where he was.

Hotel room. The Hilton. Too many free mai tais. Rum gave him a killer headache every time.

He pushed himself off the sofa and that's when he remembered Maggie. The thought spun him around to look back at the bedroom. Awake, he realized the pounding came from the front door of the suite, not the bedroom.

Platt grabbed his shirt from a nearby chair but didn't bother with his shoes. It was probably just hotel staff. He noticed the telephone's flashing red button. He didn't remember the phone ringing but he could have missed it.

By the time he opened the door he had his shirt on but not buttoned. The black man in a green polo shirt looked puzzled.

'Yes?' Platt asked.

The man stared at him, backed up and checked the number beside the doorframe, then looked over Platt's shoulder to get a glimpse inside. Not much success. He was shorter than Platt

'I'm looking for Maggie O'Dell.'

'Are you from the hotel?'

'Ah, no. Homeland Security.'

'Door-to-door check?'

'Excuse me?'

'Do we need to leave?'

'Is Maggie here?'

'Charlie?' Maggie called from behind Platt

With a glance over his shoulder, Platt saw her come out of the bathroom. Her hair was wet and she wore one of the hotel's white robes. The fresh scent of soap wafted through the entry and as distracting as it was, Platt couldn't take his eyes off Charlie, whose eyes had widened. His jaw hung open. It was classic.

'I'm sorry,' Platt said. 'You're Charlie Wurth. When you said Homeland Security, I thought you were here to tell us that we had to leave. I'm Benjamin Platt.'

He held his hand out and waited while Wurth processed the information, still trying to figure out what he was seeing. Platt spotted the paper bag in Wurth's right hand. He could smell the pastry as Wurth moved it to his left hand in order to shake.

'Come on in, Charlie. Keep Ben company while I put on some clothes,' Maggie told him. 'I overslept.' Then to Platt and with a smile, she said, 'I actually slept.'

'I'll bet,' Platt heard Wurth say, but under his breath.

Maggie was already headed through the bedroom door and Platt swore he saw a bit of a skip in her step.

FORTY-SEVEN

The sky looked as dark and murky as Scott felt. He'd taken a long shower because for some reason he could smell decomposing flesh almost as if the scent had been smeared on his skin. He put on crisply pressed trousers and shirt. No tie today. He ate breakfast with Trish. She'd prepared blueberry pancakes and sausage. She was in a good mood. Go figure.

As soon as he got in his Lexus he could smell it again. There was no mistaking the scent of decomposing flesh.

At the first intersection he pulled to the side of the road, got out, and started searching the vehicle. A splash of gasoline and a smudge of oil dirtied the plastic he'd laid in back before transporting the generator, but there was nothing else. He kept his vehicles as spotless as the funeral home.

He tried to ignore the smell. Get his mind

off it. He turned up the local radio station.

'Isaac's coming, folks. The Weather Channel's Jim Cantore was reporting from our own Pensacola Beach this morning. The eye of the storm is about a hundred miles away. Winds at 160 miles per hour. That's a cat 5, and this thing is in warm open water with nothing to slow it down. In fact, it's picked up speed and is moving at fourteen miles per hour instead of ten. That means it'll be sooner than later. We'll be seeing the outer bands about noon and this monster will be making landfall sometime tonight.

'City commissioners for Escambia and Santa Rosa counties have declared a state of emergency and shelters across both counties will start opening this morning. I'll be giving you their locations in just a minute. Folks, we're getting a big piece of this storm, and it's looking more and more like we'll be in the northeast quadrant. That means it'll be bad. Really bad.'

Scott shut it off. Hell, at least he'd be ready. He was exhausted but he was back in control.

Earlier he'd received yet another phone call from Uncle Mel's family. Now they wanted to wait until after the storm.

'Is that okay? Will he be okay?' they had asked, but Scott could tell Uncle Mel was no longer their priority. There was a storm to survive. Funny, he thought, how the dead are forgotten when the business of living distracts us.

At least they weren't forgotten by Joe Black. Again, there were no signs of a vehicle but Scott could tell from the alarm system that Joe was still inside. Where the hell did he park? There was an apartment parking lot on the other side of the trees, but he'd have to walk through the brush and tall grass that separated the two properties. And when did he start dumping his coolers in Scott's shed? Liz seemed just a little too interested. Is that where he had first started smelling decomposing flesh? Had Liz smelled it last night?

Scott walked through the back door and the scent was even stronger. He caught himself cringing. What had Joe left for him today?

'Hey, buddy.' Joe came down the hall from the walk-in refrigerator.

Scott noticed empty hands and no splatters. He restrained a sigh of relief. Instead, he glanced into the embalming room. Clean. So what was he smelling?

'I probably won't see you until after the storm,' Joe told him, slinging a backpack over his shoulder.

'Making a run for it?'

Joe laughed. 'You might say that. I have one more pickup and then I want to get my boat out of harm's way.'

'You have a boat?'

'I told you that.'

But Scott knew he hadn't. He would have remembered.

'Makes it a lot easier,' Joe explained, 'to get around afterward when the roads and bridges are out. But I need to move and dock it at least a hundred miles west of here.'

'Biloxi? New Orleans?'

'In that vicinity.'

'I just heard it's moving in a lot faster than they predicted.'

'Gotta go, then. I'll see you in a couple of days.'

Scott watched him leave and found himself wishing Joe had invited him along. Then he started hunting for the source of the smell. At one point he even sniffed himself, pulling his shirt open and taking an inside whiff. He checked the walk-in refrigerator but the scent didn't grow stronger. Maybe once he got to work he would be able to ignore it.

He rolled out a stainless-steel table with the cardboard box containing Uncle Mel. He still needed to embalm the guy. Just as well do it before the storm. He'd sold the family an expensive casket even though they didn't want it open for the memorial. Actually, the expensive sell was always easier with families that didn't want a traditional viewing. It was their way of compensating for their guilt of not wanting to take one last look.

Scott arranged everything he needed in the embalming room. He gowned up and opened the cardboard box, ready to begin.

'That son of a bitch.'

Uncle Mel's knees were cut away and both of his hands were missing.

FORTY-EIGHT

From the bedroom balcony Maggie could see that things had changed drastically overnight. The waves churned higher, crashing farther up the shore. The sky had turned into a thick gray ceiling, several layers of clouds, low and moving, each layer at its own speed. Not even noon and the heat was stifling, the humidity oppressive. She had just dried her hair and it was already damp. Her shirt stuck to her skin.

She found Platt and Wurth in the suite's living room, eating doughnuts. One of them had made coffee and the scent filled the room. Before she had a chance to sit, Platt was up getting her a Diet Pepsi from the minibar while Wurth unwrapped a chocolate doughnut to set in front of her. She held back a smile as well as any comments about the men waiting on her.

'Outer bands may start hitting the area as soon as one this afternoon,' Wurth updated her. 'Landfall is definitely gonna be tonight. Probably after dark.'

'Isn't that sooner than predicted?' Maggie asked.

'Yep. Storm's picked up a little speed. No more islands to slow it down.'

Platt had stayed drinking his coffee near the desk and now something distracted him. Maggie saw him pick up the plastic bag she'd left on top of her file folders. He was fingering the scrap of metal inside.

'That's what the coroner plucked out of the severed foot,' she told him, looking at the doughnut in front of her.

She loved chocolate doughnuts but she hadn't eaten one since that day at Quantico, less than a year ago, when a box of dough-nuts had been delivered with a terrorist's note at the bottom. Charlie Wurth couldn't possibly have known when he brought over breakfast that his gesture would threaten to crack the seal on one of her leaky compart-ments. She broke the doughnut in half and took a bite.

'Oh, I almost forgot,' Platt said, pointing at the hotel phone. 'There's a message for you.'

She looked at Wurth.

'Not me. I have your cell phone. Though I understand you probably weren't answering that last night, either.'

She wanted to laugh at his insinuation but he wasn't joking. No raised eyebrow. No typical grin. Was it possible Charlie Wurth

224

was jealous? She shook the thought out of her mind, took another bite of the dough-nut, pleased that it actually tasted good to her. Then she went to check the message.

'It's Liz Bailey,' she told the men. 'I'm going to call her back on my cell.' She left them to retrieve the phone in the bedroom. She hadn't heard a ring last night. She really must have slept hard.

Before she could dial, her cell phone rang.

'This is Maggie O'Dell.'

Hesitation, then a woman's voice. 'FBI Agent O'Dell?'

'Yes.'

'I was given your number by the Escambia County sheriff.' A pause. 'About my husband. I'm sorry I didn't even tell you my name. I'm Irene Coffland.'

The torso's wife, Maggie thought before she could stop herself. But after a while it was hard to not think in those terms.

'Mrs. Coffland, thank you for calling me.'

'I don't know what I can tell you that would be of help.'

Maggie wasn't sure what Sheriff Clayton had told Mrs. Coffland. She had to know, however, that they had only a piece of him. Tough news for anyone to receive. Maggie proceeded gently.

'Can you tell me what you remember about the last few minutes before your hus-band disappeared?'

'I've already told the local authorities as well as your sheriff.'

'I'm sorry. Look, you really don't have to talk to me. I know this isn't easy.' Maggie knew that if Mrs. Coffland called her, she wanted to talk. Sometimes when you told people they don't have to, they suddenly wanted to tell you. A cheap bit of reverse psychology.

'We had driven back to our home. After the hurricane. Things were a mess. We were worried about looters.' The woman sighed. 'What a thing to worry about. Things. They're just things. We were cleaning up. Vince had just started the generator. It was getting dark. Our neighbors had returned and we were all in our backyard when we heard a boat in the bay.'

'A boat?'

'Yes. The men thought it must be looters. Vince told us to stay put. He got his rifle and headed down to the water.'

'Alone?'

'My husband was a retired police chief. Forced retirement after his heart attack. There was no question he could handle himself. And he wanted Henry to stay with Katherine and me. Everything had been so quiet but the generator made an awful lot of noise. We heard some shouts but they sounded like greetings. Definitely not a ruckus. We relaxed a bit. Thought it might just be another neighbor. Maybe the authorities. He was gone ten, fifteen minutes. Then we heard the boat start up again. We waited for Vince.'

Another pause; this time Maggie could hear her clearing her throat. 'He never came back. We looked all night. Called the local authorities. After the storm they had too many other important things to do. So many people were unaccounted for. My husband simply became just one of dozens.'

'Did you ever find out if the authorities had a boat in your area?'

'No, they said they didn't. But I will tell you this, Vince would have fought hard if he thought whoever was on that boat was a threat to any of us.'

'I'm not sure I understand what you're saying, Mrs. Coffland.'

'We heard what sounded like greetings. An amicable exchange. Vince either recognized the person on that boat or he didn't feel threatened by him.'

As Maggie ended the call she considered what she'd learned. Vince Coffland's killer had access to or owned a boat. Probably one small enough to trailer. That would explain how Vince Coffland disappeared off the Atlantic coast and ended up in the Gulf of Mexico. She could check the Pensacola Beach marina, though without a name or even a description of the boat she knew she wouldn't have much luck.

She punched in the number for Liz Bailey as she heard a phone ring in the other room. Platt answered his phone as Liz Bailey answered Maggie.

'Hello.'

'Liz, it's Maggie O'Dell. Sorry for not getting back to you sooner.'

'Actually, I'm not sure if this means anything but I saw an exact replica of that fishing cooler we found in the Gulf.'

'Wasn't it pretty standard? Especially down here.'

'It wasn't just the cooler. It had the exact same tie-down.'

'Are you sure?'

'Looked like it. Same blue-and-yellow strands. Same thickness.'

Maggie hesitated. Could it be a coincidence? Her old boss, Assistant Director Cunningham, used to tell her there was no such thing as a coincidence. There was a very good chance that the person who owned this cooler also owned the one found in the Gulf.

Before Maggie responded, Liz continued. 'What sort of got my attention was where I saw it. You know, considering what we found inside the first one.'

'Where exactly *did* you see it?'

'In a shed back behind a funeral home.'

FORTY-NINE

Platt answered his phone, still focused on the bit of metal inside the plastic bag.

'Colonel Platt, this is Captain Ganz.'

Platt stopped. 'Captain Ganz.' He couldn't think of anything else to say to the man. Fortunately he didn't have to reply.

'I owe you an apology, Colonel.'

Silence. Perhaps he wanted it to sink in.

'You found something?'

'The other two soldiers who died last week also show traces of *Clostridium sordellii*. We've started testing the other patients. So far, nine out of ten have the bacterium. We're still not quite sure where or how it got into their bodies, but you must be right. It has to be through the bone grafts or bone paste. Right now I need to save these soldiers.'

More silence. Platt waited it out.

'Ben, I've been a jackass in the way I treated you. If you haven't left Pensacola yet, would you consider coming back and giving me a hand?'

Platt didn't hesitate. 'Of course.'

'This hurricane won't be a party. We have generators but not for everything.'

'I understand.'

229

'And we don't have the antibiotics we need.'

'This isn't your ordinary bacterium.'

'Tell me where you are and I'll have my driver pick you up.'

'He can pick me up at the Hilton. Have him ring me twice when he gets here and I'll meet him in the lobby.'

Platt got off the phone just as Maggie returned.

'You're leaving. Going back.' She said it with no hint of surprise.

'Yes. Sometimes there's no pleasure in being right.'

'You got that right,' Wurth said, getting up, ready to leave.

'I'm going to stay on the beach this morning,' Maggie told Wurth.

'That's not a good idea.' He looked at Platt. 'Tell her that's not a good idea.'

Platt shrugged. 'What makes you think she'll listen to me?'

'They'll be closing Bob Sykes Bridge,' Wurth told her, 'and the Navarre Bridge at one o'clock. There's no other way off Pensacola Beach.'

'It's okay. Liz Bailey promised I'd have a way off.'

'And what, might I ask, is it you hope to accomplish by staying?'

'Come on, Charlie, you brought me down here for a case. You can't blame me for wanting to do some footwork.'

'Speaking of foot' – Platt held out the plastic bag with the metal bit – 'I think I know what this is. It's shrapnel.'

Maggie took the bag and looked at it again. 'As in shrapnel from an explosive?'

He nodded. 'I've removed my share of this stuff from soldiers in Afghanistan. I've been staring at this piece for the last hour trying to figure out how it ended up in a severed foot found in the Gulf of Mexico.'

FIFTY

Liz came down the steps from her bedroom and dropped her duffel bag in the foyer. She was about to tap on the master-bedroom door to say goodbye to her dad when she heard him in the kitchen. She found him down on his knees, rummaging through one of the lower cabinets. He had food packages scattered on the floor around him. And more surprising, he was dressed in his navy jumpsuit, his canteen uniform.

'Dad, what are you doing?'

'Oh, hello, darlin'. I didn't wake you, did I?'

'No, I'm on my way out. I thought you'd be still sleeping.'

'Here they are,' he said as he pulled out a

box. He stood and wiped at his knees while he handed her the box of power bars. 'These are supposed to be really good. Lots of protein. They aren't the cheap ones. Throw a few in your bag. Take the box if you have room.'

She took the box and watched him stuff the other packages back into the cabinet.

'You dug through the cabinet just for these?'

'I know they'll probably have MREs for you but they get old fast. I bought these last week thinking you'd like them.'

Liz wondered if he was simply avoiding the subject of last night. Maybe he didn't remember. She wouldn't embarrass him.

'When did you get your car?'

So he did remember.

'Last night. Scott took me back to the beach.'

'Scott?'

'He was here picking up the generator you loaned him.'

Walter stared at her. 'I know I had a bit to drink yesterday, but I haven't talked to Scott in over a week.'

'Are you sure? Maybe he talked to you while you were at the Tiki Bar.'

'Nope. Had a few drinks with a friend of his from out of town.' He closed the cabinet and started pulling items from the refrigerator. 'Nice enough but a strange young fellow. Told me his daddy's name is Phillip Norris but he calls himself Joe Black. Now why would a boy not use his daddy's name?'

'Maybe his mom and dad weren't married. He told you he's a friend of Scott's?'

'No, not exactly.' He started searching through another cabinet, this time pulling out a small blender. 'He said it was nice to be drinking with someone he liked. Said that he'd spent the last two evenings on the beach with a business associate who was a – okay, now this is his word, not mine – he said he was a dickhead funeral director. Doesn't that sound like Scott? You saw Scott drunk the other night on the beach. It has to be Scott.'

Liz wondered if Joe Black was the friend of Scott's who owned the fishing cooler. Didn't he say it belonged to his friend Joe?

Her dad was gathering and arranging an array of items on the countertop: a banana, a bottle of honey, a jug of orange juice, and a carton of milk.

'What are you making here, Dad?'

'Oh, just something. I've got a little bit of a headache.'

'Like a hangover?'

He frowned and she let it go.

'You're not taking the canteen to the beach today, are you?'

'Just for an hour or two.'

'Dad, they're closing the Bob Sykes Bridge

at one.'

'I'll be gone by then. Right now there'll be some hungry people on the beach. And I need to check on some friends.'

'Promise me you'll be back here by noon.'

He nodded. 'So I won't see you until after the storm?'

'I'll call and let you know when we get to Jacksonville. We'll be doing search and rescue until they tell us to get to safety. I'm thinking that'll be sometime this afternoon.'

'You be careful. No hotdogging.'

'You be careful, too, hot-dog man.'

He smiled and shrugged.

'I'll talk to you later.' Liz kissed him on the cheek as he splashed milk and orange juice together into the blender. She thought the concoction actually looked too good to cure a hangover.

'I can't believe Scott helped himself to one of my generators without asking.'

'Sorry, Dad. He made it sound like he'd talked to you.'

She grabbed the box of power bars, and as she headed out the door she heard her dad say, 'He really is a dickhead.'

FIFTY-ONE

Maggie thought Charlie Wurth was being a bit overprotective. She knew he felt responsible for bringing her to Florida in the middle of the storm, so she wasn't surprised that all the way out her hotel door and down the hall he ranted about her staying on the beach. In fact, she could hear him still mumbling as he got on the elevator.

What she wasn't prepared for was Platt's reaction.

'You really can't stay on the beach,' he told her almost as soon as she closed the door.

'I'll be with the United States Coast Guard.'

He didn't smile.

'Really, I'll be okay,' she said.

'When the outer bands start, there'll be torrential downpours, thunderstorms, possibly tornadoes. Have you ever been in a hurricane before?'

'No, but I've been in a tunnel dug under a graveyard with a serial killer.'

'This isn't funny.'

'I wasn't being funny.' She stood back and looked at him. She'd seen his serious side, the concerned doctor watching over his patient.

235

This was something different. 'I can take care of myself.'

'I know you can.'

He let out a deep breath and rubbed at his jaw, an exhausted mannerism Maggie recognized. It only occurred to her now that he may not have gotten as much sleep as she did last night. She'd been surprised, maybe disappointed, to wake up and not find him beside her.

'I worry about you,' he said.

She started to smile until she saw the look on his face. This wasn't an easy admission for him. They teased each other a lot, but this was serious.

'I really can take care of myself,' she tried again.

'But somehow you manage to get in the way of suitcase bombs and the Ebola virus. Not to mention serial killers.'

'You're the one going off on secret missions to undisclosed locations.' Maggie's sudden switch in tone surprised her as much as it did Platt.

This time, however, he smiled and said, 'So you worry about me, too?'

She shrugged then nodded.

'It's annoying, isn't it?' He was back to teasing. A more comfortable place for both of them.

His phone rang twice and stopped. He glanced down at the number.

'My ride's here.' But he didn't move. 'Call me. Or text me. Let me know you're safe.'

'Absolutely. You do the same.'

He picked up his duffel bag and slung it over his shoulder. He started for the door, then without warning he turned back.

'What the hell,' he mumbled and in three steps he was kissing her, one hand cupping the back of her neck, the other keeping his duffel bag from banging her shoulder. 'Make sure you take care of yourself, Maggie O'Dell.'

She was glad he sounded a little out of breath. As he headed for the door another damned phone started ringing. It was Maggie's. She wanted to ignore it.

Platt smiled at her as he closed the door. 'You better get that.'

She was shaking her head then realized she was smiling, too.

'Maggie O'Dell,' she answered.

'Yes, Ms. O'Dell, this is Lawrence Piper returning your call.'

Platt had made her forget her case. It took her a second to remember who Lawrence Piper was and why she had called him.

'You wanted to know about a delivery,' he prompted.

How could she play this? She couldn't very well tell him she'd found his phone number on a label stuck to a cooler full of body parts. Or could she?

'Concerning Destin on August twenty-fourth,' she said, just as she realized the twenty-fourth was yesterday.

'I don't understand. I told Joe we had to cancel Destin because of the hurricane.'

He sounded like a businessman. She hadn't had the chance to research Advanced Medical Educational Technology. But there was nothing clandestine or sinister in his tone. The best interrogators Maggie had worked with had taught her that the less the interrogator said, the more the interrogated filled in. She waited.

'Are you working with Joe?' Piper asked.

'I'm trying to.' She kept her remarks innocuous.

Piper laughed and added, 'I told him he needed an assistant. Look, Maggie – you don't mind if I call you Maggie.'

A businessman but also a salesman, Maggie decided.

'Not at all.'

'I already told Joe I'd make this cancellation up to him. I've got a couple dozen surgeons coming to a conference in Tampa over Labor Day. I'm going to need at least twenty-two cervical spines. I'd prefer brain with skull base intact, if that's possible.'

Maggie thought about the body parts found in the cooler, individually wrapped in plastic. Could it be that simple? A body broker making a delivery? From what little she knew, there was nothing illegal about it. Most federal regulations applied only to organs. Few states regulated anything beyond that.

'I don't want to lose Joe,' he said when she didn't respond. Evidently Maggie's silence was disconcerting to Piper. 'Can you tell him that? He hasn't called and the number I have for him has already been changed. That's an annoying habit your new boss has.'

'Yes, I know. He likes to be the one calling.' She wasn't surprised.

'It's tough to find someone with his skill and consistency. Especially someone who delivers and sets up. Can you tell him that?'

'Yes,' Maggie said.

As she pressed End, she noticed she had missed a call: Dr. Tomich.

Brokered body parts. It made sense. And it probably explained the identical cooler Liz Bailey saw outside a funeral home. It didn't, however, explain Vince Coffland's disappearance.

Maggie pressed Return Call.

'Tomich,' he snapped. His clipped manner made his name sound as if it were a swear word.

'Dr. Tomich, it's Maggie O'Dell returning your call.'

'Ah yes. Agent O'Dell.'

Before she could tell him that the parts might be brokered, Tomich surprised her by

239

saying, 'It appears you were correct.'

'Excuse me?'

'After examining the X-rays I discovered a bullet in Mr Vince Coffland.'

'Are you certain it wasn't shrapnel? I think that's what the metal is in the severed foot.'

'No, no, no. This is a bullet. I went back and extracted it. Looks like a .22 caliber handgun. The trajectory path would suggest that it entered somewhere below the occipital bone and above the cervical vertebrae.'

'In other words he was shot in the back of the head.'

'That would be within the broad range, yes. You understand I am speculating. Without the head and neck I do not have the entrance wound. But from where the bullet was lodged and from the downward path it left in the tissue, I would estimate that the victim may have been bending over when shot.'

Execution style? Maggie kept the thought to herself as she thanked Dr. Tomich and ended the call.

The body parts might have actually been meant for one of AMET's surgical conferences. However, it looked like Piper's connection, Joe the body broker, might also be a killer.

FIFTY-TWO

Charlotte Mills packed up the last plastic container and hauled it upstairs. She had secured all her important documents, jewelry, and memorabilia, including photo albums, scrapbooks, and her collection of autographed novels. One container alone held all the newspaper and magazine articles about her husband's 'untimely death,' or as Charlotte called it, his Mafia-style murder.

The federal government had ruled the plane crash an accident, an unfortunate engine failure on the Lear jet that was supposed to deliver him to Tallahassee so he could testify in front of a grand jury. She had warned George months before that turning state's evidence could mean his death. But he insisted it was the right thing to do, his penance for helping 'the son-of-a-bitch' corrupt politician get elected. As a result, the son of a bitch kept his job.

That was fifteen years ago and Charlotte Mills had gotten nowhere in her diligent pursuit of the truth. Five years ago she gave up – or at least, that's what it felt like, when, in fact, she had depleted all of her options. She didn't want also to deplete her financial resources. George would have been furious with her if she had done that. So finally she accepted the life-insurance money, the policy that George had invested in just months before the grand jury convened.

She had already quit her job to work full-time investigating George's murder. It turned out to be way too many wasted hours. When she finally stopped, she bought this place on the beach, and now she spent her days walking along the shore collecting shells. And she spent her nights reading all the wonderful novels she hadn't had time for. It wasn't a bad life and she wasn't going to let some hurricane dismantle it.

Charlotte took a long, hot shower, knowing it might be her last for a week. She put on comfy clothes, tied her short gray hair into a stubby ponytail. She checked her list as she placed new batteries in a variety of flashlights. She filled the bathtub, all the sinks, and the washing machine with water. She stuffed extra bottled water into the freezer. The latter was a small trick she'd learned during the last hurricane threat. It meant having ice to keep things cool and water to drink later.

With the windows and patio door boarded up the house was dark, reminding her that she'd need to put the candles and matches in a plastic bag and have them somewhere she could grab when the electricity went off.

Same for the extra batteries.

Her master bathroom was the only true inside room and she had set it up as her refuge. The counter was arranged with the necessities: a battery-operated radio, several flashlights, a telephone already plugged into a landline, a cooler filled with sandwiches, her prescription meds, and even a pickax almost too large for her small frame to lift. Everything she would need for a ten- to twelve-hour stay.

She was on her way back upstairs when a knock at the front door stopped her. The sheriff's department had come by earlier. Her neighbors had already left. She checked the peephole. Saw the patch on the man's sleeve and she let out a groan. Was this the county or the federal government's last-ditch effort?

'I already told the sheriff's deputy that I was staying,' she insisted as she opened the door only to the security chain's length.

'Hi, Mrs. Mills,' the young man said with a smile. 'I met you at Mr. B's yesterday. Joe. Joe Black.'

FIFTY-THREE

Walter parked the canteen as close to the marina as possible. That's where all the action was this morning. They warned him at the tollbooth that the bridge would be closing at one o'clock. Traffic was bumper-to-bumper in the opposite direction. He realized he probably should have stayed home, found something to occupy his time, but he had everything ready and there was only so much you could prepare. He didn't want to sit at home and wait. There'd be enough waiting while the storm raged on for hours.

The marina was crowded with last-minute boaters trying to tether their boats – big and small – as best as possible. Some were loading their crafts onto trailers. A few brave souls – or stupid, Walter decided – were venturing out into the swell in an attempt to get their boats out of the storm's path.

Tension filled the air along with diesel fumes. Arguments edged close to fistfights. The waiting and watching of the last several days ended with the inevitable realization that Isaac was, indeed, heading directly for them. There was no more predicting. No more hope for a last-minute turn. There was no more escaping. Now it was only a matter of battening down the hatches as best as possible.

Walter parked in a corner of the marina lot where the boaters could see him and he could chat with them. Howard Johnson, the owner of the marina and a deep-sea fishing shop, had invited Walter to set up here anytime he wanted. In exchange Walter kept a special bottle of cognac so at the end of a hard day he and Howard could sip and share stories.

Walter decided that today he'd only stay an hour. He'd serve up whatever he had on board for free until the food or the hour ran out.

At first he didn't pay attention to the panel van that pulled up next to the sidewalk leading to the docks. He noticed the owner struggling with a huge bag, yanking it out of the van then dragging it. Not an unusual scene down here. Walter had seen this type of bag before. Someone had pointed one out, calling it a 'tuna bag.' Fishermen used them for the big catches that didn't fit in a cooler. The bags were tough, huge, waterproof, and insulated. About six feet by three feet it looked like a giant-size tote bag with a washable lining that could be removed.

Walter thought it was a bit odd that someone would be hauling a fish to his boat. Usually it was the other way around. The guy wore a blue baseball cap, shorts, deck shoes, and a khaki button-down shirt with the tails untucked. Walter caught a glimpse of the chevron patch on the shirt sleeve. What the hell was some navy petty officer doing here in his service uniform, dragging a tuna bag? Then Walter recognized the guy.

'Hey, Joe.'

Too much noise. Joe didn't hear him.

That bag looked awful heavy.

Walter glanced around inside the canteen. He hadn't turned on any appliances yet. He left a tray with hot dogs and condiments out. He'd be right back. Then he locked all the doors and headed over to the sidewalk to help.

'Hey, Norris.'

This time Joe looked over his shoulder and did a double take. His face was red and dripping sweat. His eyes darted around the marina like he hadn't expected to be recognized.

'Let me give you a hand with that,' Walter said, grabbing one end of the bag.

'No, that's okay, Mr. B. I've got it.'

Joe tried to pull away but Walter didn't surrender his end. Instead, he asked, 'You got a boat out here?' He really wanted to ask why Joe was wearing what was probably one of his father's old shirts. Even his ball cap had the U.S. Navy insignia embroidered on the front. Walter waited till Joe gave up and let him help.

'Cabin cruiser.' Joe nodded at the boat in the second slip to their right.

Walter whistled. 'She's a beauty.' He smiled at the name, bold and black, written across the stern: *Restless Sole*.

'My dad left it to me. Thought I'd take it over to Biloxi.'

'Now? You're kidding, right?'

'The eye of the storm's probably going to come over Pensacola. Maybe swing a bit to the east of here. Hurricane-force winds stretch about a hundred miles out from the eye.' He wasn't out of breath. Walter was. He found himself thinking that this kid's in good shape.

'There's already nine-, ten-foot swells,' Walter told him, trying not to gasp like an old man.

'I've been out in worse. Northeast quadrant gets the worst part of the storm. Traveling west I'll be driving away from it. Got a little delayed. I'm getting a later start than I wanted.'

Walter helped Joe lift the bag onto the boat deck. By now, Walter's jumpsuit was soaked at his back and chest. Sweat poured down his forehead and dripped off his nose, but he needed both hands to lift his end of the tuna bag down the steps into the cabin.

Joe dropped his end of the bag. Something inside moved and groaned. Walter's eyes shot up to meet Joe's. He was still holding

247

his end of the bag when Joe shoved the snub nose of a revolver into Walter's gut and said, 'Guess you're coming along for the ride, Mr. B.'

FIFTY-FOUR

Maggie knew if she waited until after the hurricane to ask questions no one would remember a white stainless-steel cooler with a bright yellow-and-blue tie-down or its owner, a guy named Joe, who might have a boat docked at the marina. Memories of before the hurricane would be eclipsed by the chaos of the storm. Besides, she had promised Liz Bailey that she would meet her on the marina. While she waited, she might just as well ask some questions.

The condition of the body parts suggested they hadn't been in the cooler for long. Decomposition had only begun. From past experience – an unfortunate piece of trivia to have in one's repertoire – Maggie knew it took about four to five hours to thaw an average-size frozen torso. There had been no ice left in the cooler when it was found. Considering the warm water of the Gulf and the hot sun, she estimated the packages had been inside the cooler two days. Three at the most.

Even if the body parts had been destined for one of Lawrence Piper's surgical conferences, it still didn't explain how Vince Coffland ended up as an unwilling body donor.

Before Maggie had left the comfort of her hotel room she had done a quick search of Advanced Medical Educational Technology on her laptop. The company advertised educational seminars at a variety of Florida resorts, providing a venue for medical-device makers to showcase their latest technologies to surgeons from across the country. They promised hands-on experience while upholding donor confidentiality by not disclosing their procurement procedure.

After viewing competitors' websites, Maggie realized AMET was only one of several legitimate companies buying 'precut and frozen body parts' from brokers like Joe. From her quick analysis, Maggie understood that demand was high and supply limited. She couldn't help wondering if Platt had been right when he asked if this killer might be taking advantage of hurricanes in order to find victims. Now Maggie realized that might be exactly what this killer was doing, using the storms as a cover to fill his growing orders. Was Vince Coffland murdered out of cold-blooded greed?

The marina was crowded and the shops were busy, trying to accommodate the desperate boat owners. In between sales Maggie struck up a conversation with the owner of Howard's Deep Sea Fishing Shop. A huge, barrel-chested man, Howard Johnson towered over Maggie. His thick white hair was the only indication of his age. Somewhere in his sixties, Maggie guessed. However, his neatly trimmed goatee had streaks of blond, hinting at the golden-haired surfer that appeared in the photos along the walls. He wore a bright orange-and-blue button-down shirt with a fish pattern, the hem hanging over his khaki cargo shorts.

His shop was kept neat, with unusual and colorful gear. A railed shelf ran along the upper quarter of the four walls, filled with models of various boats and ships. Maggie found herself mesmerized by all the paraphernalia.

Her eyes were still darting about as she absently flipped open her FBI badge to show Howard. His entire demeanor changed. He nodded politely but his eyes flashed with suspicion. One large hand ducked into his pocket, the other dropped palm-flat onto the counter as if bracing himself for what was coming. Okay, so he didn't trust FBI agents. He wouldn't be the first. Maggie showed him photos of the cooler. The last one was a close-up of the yellow-and-blue rope tie-down.

He shrugged. 'Looks like a dozen other coolers I see every day. In fact, I have this same make, only the larger version, on my deep-sea fishing rig.'

'What about the tie-down?'

'I use a metal one.'

'Ever see one like this?'

Another shrug but he looked at the photo again. She could see he was still suspicious. He crossed his arms over his barrel chest. Guarded. An impatient frown.

'People use all sorts of things to personalize their equipment,' he said. 'Makes it easier to pick it out when everybody's unloading their stuff on the dock at the same time. Kind of like baggage claim. You know what I mean? People tag their bags with ribbons or bright straps so they can see them coming down the conveyor belt.'

Maggie hadn't thought of that. Using the rope to track down the killer started looking like a million-to-one shot.

'Any ideas how a cooler this size would end up overboard?'

'You mean by accident?'

She nodded.

Howard's frown screwed up his face and he scratched his head like he was giving it considerable thought.

'Sometimes guys will pull them behind the boat when they're a bit crowded on board. They float no matter what they have in them. You tether them real good to the back of the boat. I suppose one could break loose.

Might not notice until you've gone a ways.'

'Maggie.'

It was Liz Bailey. They'd planned to meet on the marina, but Liz came into the shop in a rush.

'Howard, have you seen my dad?'

FIFTY-FIVE

Benjamin Platt held the young man by the shoulders as he vomited green liquid into a stainless-steel basin. The patient was too weak to hold himself up. That was obvious from the stains already on his bedsheets.

'We're going to give you an injection,' he told the soldier as he eased him back down. The man's eyes were glazed. He no longer tried to respond. Platt knew he probably couldn't hear him, but he talked to him anyway.

He nodded for the nurse beside him to go ahead with the injection while he explained. 'We'll probably be poking you a couple more times.' Platt grabbed a towel from the side stand and wiped vomit from the corner of the young man's mouth.

'Thanks.'

The one word seemed an effort so Platt was surprised when he continued.

252

'This is almost worse' – he slurred his syllables – 'than losing my foot.'

'It's going to get better,' Platt told him. 'I promise you.' The nurse looked skeptical. He could see her out of the corner of his eye but Platt didn't break eye contact with the young man. He would not let him see that even his doctor wasn't sure what would work.

Platt stopped at the prep room to change gloves before he went on to the next patient.

'Controlled chaos,' Ganz said coming up behind him.

'Controlled being the key word.'

'I have someone bringing in more beta-lactam antibiotics. You think this will work?'

'Think of *Clostridium sordellii* as tiny egg-like spores. They have to chew away enzymes for their bacterial cell wall to synthesize. This group of antibiotics binds to those enzymes and makes them inactivate, or at least not available to the bacteria.'

'So it won't be able to grow.'

'Or spread.'

'What about those patients where it's already spread?'

Platt took in a deep breath. 'I don't know. I honestly don't know. There is no established treatment. We're shooting from the hip here.' He turned to look Ganz in the eyes. 'Are you having second thoughts?'

'No, absolutely not.' He shook his head. 'At this point we don't have anything to lose.'

'This will slow the bacteria down even in those advanced cases. It'll really depend on what damage has already been done.' Platt's mind looped back to what the young man had said about this being worse than losing his foot. 'What do you do with the amputated limbs?'

'Excuse me?'

'The young man I just took care of – what happened to his foot once it was amputated?'

'Some families request the limbs. Others go to the tissue bank.'

'In Jacksonville?'

'Right.'

'What if the limb has shrapnel in it?'

'That's not my area of expertise.'

'But would you send it on to the tissue bank?' Platt insisted.

'Sure. That's where the assessment would be made. But shrapnel still embedded in the tissue? I think the foot would probably be considered damaged and discarded.'

Platt wondered about Maggie's case. Was it possible the severed foot that had been discovered in the fishing cooler was actually one that had been amputated from a soldier?

FIFTY-SIX

Liz's first reaction at seeing the deserted canteen had been anger. She was already frustrated with her dad for driving to the beach that morning out of boredom, curiosity. He didn't want to miss out on the action. Sometimes she wondered if she was the same way. She had his drive, that same eagerness to get out there, no matter how dangerous. Once the adrenaline kicked in, it was difficult to slow her down.

Her anger changed to concern when she glanced inside the canteen and saw the tray of hot dogs and condiments on the counter. The vehicle was locked up but it was obvious her father had intended to be away only a short time. Howard only stoked her concern.

'I saw him, maybe an hour ago. He was helping some guy drag a tuna bag onto his boat.'

'Is the boat still here?' She hated that she sounded so anxious. Even Maggie stood alongside Liz, looking out the window, appearing anxious. It was getting darker by the minute. The lights in the parking lot had started to turn on. And it wasn't even noon.

Howard glanced over the two of them.

255

'Nope. It was in slip number two.'

'It's pretty late to be moving a boat, isn't it?' Maggie asked.

'And dangerous,' Liz added.

'Actually, it's stupid, but he's not the only one,' Howard said. 'Can't tell them anything. You know the type. They'll get in trouble and expect you and your aircrew to go out and risk your lives to save their sorry asses.'

'Is that one of your slips?'

'Yep, sure is.' He was already at his computer, bringing up his accounts.

Liz had heard a lot of rumors about Howard Johnson. Word was that he had been a drug trafficker for years and that he only gave it up when he knew the feds were moving in to bust him. There were also rumors that several million dollars of drug money had never been recovered and that Howard had it hidden somewhere. But her dad always said that Howard was 'one of the good guys.'

'Boat's named *Restless Sole*, that's s-o-l-e. Owner is listed as Joe Black. He came in Friday. Has the slip through this week.'

'Maybe he took it out to get gas?' Maggie asked.

'Every place I know of is already out of gas,' Howard said. 'But maybe he knows something I don't.'

'Wait a minute,' Liz said. 'Joe Black?' She turned to Maggie. 'My dad had drinks with him last night. Dad said he was a friend of my brother-in-law's.' Panic started to twist knots in her stomach. 'Scott said he owned the fishing cooler. The one I saw behind the funeral home.'

Maggie stared at her a moment. Liz knew she could see her concern.

'Any idea where Black's from? Or where he might be headed?' Maggie asked Howard.

He glanced from Maggie to Liz and back to Maggie. Howard could see it, too. 'That might be an issue of privacy. Without a warrant I don't think I can give you his address in Jacksonville.' Then he waved at an impatient customer. 'Excuse me, ladies.'

Liz leaned closer to Maggie, keeping her back to the crowded shop. 'Dad said he didn't think Joe Black was his real name.'

'No,' Maggie said, much too calmly. 'I don't think it's his real name, either.'

'Do you think he's the owner of the cooler we found in the Gulf?'

'Yes,' she said with certainty.

'Is my dad in danger?'

'He may have just helped Black load his boat. He could be helping someone else right now.'

Liz glanced out the shop window. Her dad was in great physical shape for his age. He could handle himself. She shouldn't jump to conclusions. He probably was off helping someone else. He had been in the navy for more than thirty-five years. He knew a thing or two about securing boats.

The wind came in a sudden blast, bending palm trees and upending anything that wasn't weighted down. Buckets and empty gas cans skidded across the pier. The glass in the windows rattled. The entire shop went silent so when the rain started it sounded like stones pelting the outside walls.

The door banged open. Kesnick, wearing a bright-yellow poncho, found Liz.

'Hey Bailey, we gotta go.'

He handed the women identical ponchos still folded up in neat squares. Liz reminded herself that Maggie hadn't experienced anything like this.

'We're going up in this?' The calm was gone, replaced by anxiety.

'It's just the outer bands,' Liz told her. 'It'll calm down again in a few minutes. We'll have about six to ten hours of this, on and off. It'll quit as suddenly as it started. The intensity and length of time will increase with each round.'

She thought Maggie looked a shade paler and Liz added, 'I've got more of the ground-ginger capsules in my medic pack.'

Liz searched for Howard on their way out. Hated to take him away from a paying customer but he sensed her tension, and he didn't even wait for her question. Instead, he said, 'I'll take care of him if I find him. And don't worry about the canteen.'

FIFTY-SEVEN

The boat rolled from side to side, throwing Walter against the inside walls of the cabin. Joe Black had hog-tied Walter's hands and feet with a braided rope and left him to slide and knock against the wood panels. The tuna bag lay between him and the steps going up to the cockpit.

He tried to watch the bag, though he had to twist and look over his shoulder to see it. He couldn't turn himself around with the boat heaving him every time he made an attempt. But Walter was sure something, or rather someone, was in the bag. There had been what sounded like groans early on. Not anymore.

'How you doing, Walter?' Joe had to yell to be heard over the engine.

He poked his head down to take a peek. Walter could see only a corner of his forehead. He knew the kid didn't dare leave the cockpit. He'd have to stay put and keep his hands on the controls. From the increased tilt and raise of the boat, Walter could tell the waves were cresting even more violently. Soon it wouldn't matter how Joe steered.

He heard a crackle of static and then Joe's

voice boomed through a box on the wall, just over Walter's head.

'Hey, Walter. I know you can't hit the response button but I just wanted to explain some stuff to you. It's nothing personal. It's just business.'

Walter jerked onto his side to take a better look at the box on the wall about three feet above him. Was it an intercom or a radio? Light came in only through the portholes, which were being pummeled by waves. It was too dark for him to tell. He scooted against the wall, trying to gain leverage just as the boat lurched and threw him to the other side of the boat, knocking his head against the wall. It was enough for him to see shooting stars.

'Everything I told you, Walter, was true.' Joe's voice came through the wall. 'You know, about my dad. He was in the navy. Loved it. Even though they weren't so good to him. He didn't get this boat until he found out he was sick. Waited too long to enjoy life. Always said he couldn't afford it.'

Another wave almost capsized the boat. The tuna bag slammed into Walter. He pressed his heels into one wall and his shoulders against the other, wedging himself tight. When the boat rocked back down, the tuna bag slid toward the steps but Walter stayed put.

Something told him it was all a big roller-coaster ride to this kid. He knew guys like Joe Black in the navy. They loved the adventure, the more dangerous the better. They craved it. He recognized a bit of that in himself. He saw it in his daughter Liz, and he worried it could end up getting her hurt. There always came a time when the rush wasn't enough or when you thought you were invincible because you had survived. What was it Liz had told him they said these days? You looked the beast in the face and won? So you upped the ante, took bigger and bigger risks.

No, Walter wasn't surprised that the hurricane didn't deter Joe. A moment later he was saying, 'Hey, Walter, I wish you didn't have to be tied up, 'cause I think you'd be enjoying this. You should see it from up here. Bet you spent rougher times out on the seas, huh?' There was more static then a click-click and he thought the connection had failed.

Then Joe added, 'Might have lost you there. These radios need updating.'

Walter waited out another crest – up, up, up, and finally back down. The tuna bag rolled to one side and crashed into the other, but he stayed put.

'I learned from my dad, Walter. You can't put off living the good life. You've got to take what you can whenever you can. And after all those years when my dad got sick and the navy didn't do right by him ... well, let's just say I'm evening the score.'

Another surge.

'And you know what else, Walter? I've learned to love hurricanes. You just have to work them to your favor.'

Walter thought Joe was referring to the roller-coaster ride. It didn't occur to him what Joe meant until he saw the tuna bag moving, the zipper working its way down.

'Yup, these hurricanes have been a cash cow for me this summer. Because you know what? People disappear all the time after a hurricane. A missing person suddenly becomes a donor. You know how much one body's worth these days?'

Walter's head pounded and he blinked his eyes hard, thinking maybe he was hallucinating. He twisted and jerked around to see better, holding his breath while he watched a bruised and battered Charlotte Mills crawl out of the tuna bag.

FIFTY-EIGHT

Maggie knew she'd need more than a couple of capsules of powdered ginger to get her through this. Why had she ever thought Liz Bailey's offer of 'a ride' off Pensacola Beach would be simple? Why? Because she had no idea what to expect. What was it that she had said to Charlie Wurth yesterday? 'It's one storm. How bad can it be?'

Everyone kept calling these the 'outer bands,' but the air was already too thick to breathe. Maggie felt like the world had been tipped on its side. Trees bent sideways. The rain poured in horizontal streams. The few people outside teetered from side to side, leaning into the wind to avoid being blown over. She struggled to keep her own balance while sand pelted her skin like a million tiny pinpricks.

Then as suddenly as it began, it stopped. Maggie swore she could even see a swirl of blue sky through the layers of gray overhead. Liz had finished gearing up and was watching her.

'You gonna be okay?'

'Sure. Absolutely,' Maggie said, zipping open her flight suit just enough to show Liz her shoulder holster and Smith & Wesson tucked inside. 'I've got all the control I need,' she joked.

Liz smiled but was unsuccessful in covering her concern. It wasn't quite the same look Maggie had seen in Liz's eyes when she thought her father might be in danger. Earlier, there had been just a hint of panic and Maggie's immediate reaction was to squelch it. Truth was, Liz's father might be in danger if he was still with Joe Black, but there wasn't anything they could do about it right now.

She could tell Liz had switched into rescue mode.

'How can you be so brave?' Maggie asked her.

Liz smiled at her again until she realized Maggie wasn't joking.

'My first instinct is simply to survive.'

Maggie raised an eyebrow. She wanted to understand.

'Just because I go up in a helicopter or plunge down into the ocean doesn't make me brave. It just makes me a bit crazy.' She gave a short laugh. 'Look, I know there are things you do instinctively, too. Things that I wouldn't dare. Rescuing someone and coming face to face with a killer, in the end both those situations come down to our instinct to survive.' She shrugged. 'I don't have time to think about being brave. I bet you don't, either.'

Maggie wanted to ask her how she had gotten so wise. She realized Liz was waiting for some response, some sign of agreement or understanding. But Maggie simply nodded.

'Anyway, don't worry too much about this trip,' Liz added. 'We probably won't get any distress calls before we have to head to Jacksonville. They won't let us stay up for very long. As soon as the wind hits forty knots, we're out of here.'

But Maggie wasn't really listening any-more. She was watching out the window as Lieutenant Commander Wilson and his co-pilot, Ellis, boarded the helicopter. Pete Kes-nick was waiting for Liz and Maggie. And all Maggie could think about was how quickly the sky had turned an impossibly darker shade of gray.

FIFTY-NINE

'My God, Charlotte. Are you okay?' Walter could hardly believe his eyes.

The right side of her small face was one purple bruise. Her gray hair stuck out from her ponytail. Her lower lip was split and her eyes were wild, a combination of shock and panic. She stared at Walter as if she didn't recognize him. She crawled out of the bag, dragging her right leg. The ankle was so swollen it reminded Walter of rising bread, puffing out of her sneaker.

'Charlotte,' he whispered again.

His eyes darted to the open stairwell. Joe had gone silent on the radio. Walter wanted to believe Joe wouldn't leave the cockpit. He prayed he wouldn't leave the cockpit.

'Do you know where we are?' Walter asked.

She kicked the bag away and grabbed on

to a leather strap in the floor just as the boat pitched sideways.

Other than the bruises and the swollen ankle, Walter couldn't see any broken bones or bleeding.

'Can you hear me, Charlotte?' He kept his voice low and quiet. He knew what it could do to a person to be stuck in a hold. A bag probably had the same effect. He worried that she might be too far gone to be of any help. 'Charlotte?'

'I've heard every word that bastard said from the time he dropped me on my head.'

Walter wanted to laugh with relief. 'Good ole Charlotte.'

She crawled up beside him and started to work on his ropes but Walter stopped her.

He pointed above him with his chin. 'I can wait. Do you know how to use a two-way radio?'

SIXTY

They had only been in the air a few minutes when the distress call came in. Liz heard Wilson talking to their command post, getting the details. She glanced over at Maggie. The FBI agent had looked okay until another outer band swept in. Now she clenched the leather hold-down and tightened her seat belt.

Liz realized that being in the air, the sensation of wind and rain was different. Wilson couldn't just fly above the clouds like a jetliner and get out of it. And his tight-fisted handling of the controls made the craft rock and plunge more than necessary.

She started preparing to be deployed. From the brief description it sounded like a medical emergency. The craft, a thirty-two-foot cabin cruiser, was intact, not taking on water and not disabled. That should make things easier but not much.

The water was choppy, waves cresting nine to twelve feet.

It was crazy even for a professional to be out in this.

'Let's keep the swimmer out of the water,' Wilson said.

She was still 'the swimmer,' Liz thought and immediately knew she needed to keep her focus on the boat below. The adrenaline had already started pumping. She didn't care about Wilson.

They could see the boat, the waves tossing it, almost perpendicular to the sky. Then the waves would crest and the boat would crash down. It looked like the boat was swallowed up whole then spit out, to begin the process all over.

'Let the boat deck rise up to meet you,' Pete

Kesnick was telling Liz through her helmet. 'But get on before the wave crests. You want to hang on to something before it breaks.'

She nodded but his eyes held hers as if he needed to see for himself that she was, indeed, up to the task.

Choppy seas always made it dangerous. The wind gusts and the moving boat contributed to the challenge.

'We'll never get a basket down with these winds,' Wilson said.

'Did they say what the medical condition was?' Kesnick asked.

'No. They lost contact before giving any details.'

'We try no more than three times,' Kesnick said. He was talking to Liz. 'If I think it's not working, I'm hauling you back up. Understand?'

'No heroics, Bailey,' Wilson told her. 'We don't want to lose our rescue swimmer before the hurricane even hits.'

SIXTY-ONE

As soon as they heard the helicopter overhead Joe Black came pounding down the steps.

'What the hell did you do, Walter?'

They hadn't been able to untie the rope yet from Walter's feet. He couldn't stand up without immediately losing his balance but he swung a fist at his surprised captor, hitting Joe in the face. Charlotte scrambled to her feet, her swollen ankle making her hop as she tried to land a blow. Then the boat heaved and sent them all crashing to the deck.

When the boat steadied, Joe had Charlotte by the back of her collar and his snub-nose revolver pointed at Walter's chest.

'I knew I should have killed you both. I just didn't want you stinking up my boat by the time I got to Biloxi.'

He pushed Charlotte down onto the floor next to Walter. Then he stood over them, glancing at the steps. Walter could see he was anxious to get back up.

If the helicopter didn't see any signs of distress, would they risk sending someone down? And dear God, Walter silently prayed, please don't let it be Liz. He hoped she was already on her way to Jacksonville and this was another crew left behind for a last-minute search.

'I haven't ruled out shooting you both,' Joe was telling them. He set his feet apart and braced one hand on the wall to steady himself while the boat rocked and climbed again. 'I just hate using a gun or a knife. Damages too much tissue. There's nothing worse than a cooler full of damaged goods.'

He was ranting, and Walter wondered if his internal check-and-balance system had cracked under the stress. Madmen were dangerous. Was it too late or could he get through to the kid?

Walter pressed a hand against the wall, and tried lifting himself up to his feet.

'Just stay put, Walter, or I'll shoot you in the hand. I've got plenty hands. Once they figured out how to repair carpel tunnel, hands as a commodity went bust.'

'It's over, Phillip Norris's son,' Walter said, deliberately using his father's name.

Walter watched Joe's eyes. He wanted to bring back the boy who enjoyed Coney Island hot dogs. He was certain that if he could do that, they would be safe. He wasn't prepared for Joe's response.

Joe aimed the gun, pulled back the trigger, and Walter's left hand exploded.

SIXTY-TWO

Scott ignored Trish's phone calls. He turned the cell phone off and threw it on the embalming table.

She wanted him to get to her father's house. She couldn't find her dad. Couldn't

270

get in touch with her sister. She was panicked again. Earlier he had told her that he needed to stay at the funeral home to make sure everything was okay. If a window blew out, he wanted to be here to board it up so there wasn't any water damage. She didn't understand. After all, he hadn't lifted a finger to protect their brand-new home.

'This is different,' he tried to explain. This was their livelihood. They could stay in a hotel if their home was destroyed. But if the funeral home was damaged, they would have no money coming in. How could she not understand the difference?

He'd just finished washing his hands. He couldn't get rid of the smell of decomposing flesh. He checked cupboards. Washed down the embalming room. Sprayed disinfectants. Still the smell persisted. He'd heard about olfactory hallucinations at one of the funeral-director conferences. At the time he thought it sounded ridiculous. Now he wondered if, in fact, that's what was happening to him.

Outside the world grew dark. Power lines danced in the wind. The sporadic downpours left water flooding the streets. Pine trees had already snapped in half. With every wave, the storm grew more intense. From the radio Scott learned that once the hurricane made landfall there would be no break for six to ten hours. Twelve to fifteen if the backstorm was just as intense.

He had to admit, now that he'd seen a piece of the pre-storm, he was frightened. As a kid he had fought claustrophobia after being locked inside the trunk of a neighbor's car – his punishment for mouthing off to the older, stronger kids. This storm renewed his claustrophobia.

A crash brought him to the window.

'Son of a bitch.'

A branch from the huge live oak outside the back door had been ripped off. The heavy part tumbled to the ground but power lines held up the other end. Sparks flashed. The lights in the funeral home blinked a couple of times but stayed on.

He realized the tree could end up coming through the roof. If windows exploded and branches flew in, he might not be safe inside. Trish had said that earlier, but he hadn't listened.

He grabbed a flashlight and started looking for cover. The utility closet? On the radio they had said an interior room with no windows was best. He paced the hallway. Then suddenly he stopped and turned around.

Why hadn't he thought of it sooner? The walk-in refrigerator was stainless steel. Nothing could rip that apart.

He turned on the light and pulled a chair inside. He shoved the table with Uncle Mel to one side. Joe Black had left two shelves filled with body parts. The other table was still occupied by the young man that Scott had imagined moved.

He closed the walk-in refrigerator's door and made himself sit down. This was perfect. No way this hurricane would touch him.

The lights blinked again. He heard a click, followed by two more. The electronic locks on the walk-in refrigerator's door had just engaged. He raced to the door just as the lights went out. His stomach sank. He wouldn't be able to open the door until the electricity came back on.

SIXTY-THREE

Liz wiped at her goggles. It didn't help. Just as she could see, the spray clouded her sight, again.

The wind yanked her up and down, whipping her from side to side. Once she almost made contact and Kesnick pulled too far up. Finally, her feet hit the deck. Kesnick slackened the cable. She dropped and rolled as a wave swallowed the boat. It almost pushed her overboard. She felt the cable go taut just as she grabbed on to a railing. Before Kesnick could change his mind, Liz waved that she was okay.

Communication would be tough. Almost impossible. Her hand gestures might become invisible as the rain intensified. But if the boat swirled out of control, she was still connected to the helicopter. And at the first sign of trouble Kesnick would pull her up.

She crawled along the deck, grabbing on to hooks and cables attached to the boat. She couldn't see anyone at the helm. She focused on her task. She was in control. There was no room for panic.

Liz pulled at the cabin door. The wind fought her. She hung on and ducked just as another wave came crashing over the top. The hoist cable tugged at her waist. Kesnick was impatient, nervous. She took the time to wave up at him. Could he see her thumbs-up?

The time between crests grew shorter. She had maybe a dozen seconds. She yanked at the cabin door again, using all her strength. It popped open.

No one was at the wheel. The engines were turned off. The owner must have realized there was no fighting the waves.

'Hello,' she yelled and stood still, listening for a response.

Nothing. Static behind her. The radio.

'Anyone down there?'

She pulled off her goggles. Let them dangle around her neck. She waited to catch

274

her breath then she started down the steps.

The gun was pressed against her left temple before she even saw it.

SIXTY-FOUR

'She's in,' Pete Kesnick said, but Maggie didn't hear any relief in his words. If anything, he sounded more on edge. Their swimmer was out of sight and they still didn't have any idea what the situation was down below.

'If the medical condition or injury is serious, she may not be able to use the quick strop.' Kesnick practically hung out the open doorway. He leaned against his own cable, fighting the rain and wind, trying to watch for Liz.

He had double-checked the cable. A good thing, because Maggie was certain she wouldn't be able to help this time. Not with the wind violently shoving the helicopter around. The roar made it difficult to hear even the voices inside her helmet.

'She's gonna need to hurry.' Wilson sounded as tightly wound as the cable. 'We gotta go. Command center is telling me ten minutes. Tops.'

'We can't do this in ten minutes,' Kesnick told him. 'She might be stabilizing someone

275

on board.'

'I'm watching the clock. That's all I'm saying.'

'Can someone go down and help her?' Maggie asked.

Silence. It was as if they didn't want to acknowledge her presence. Wilson had already put up a fuss about her being on his craft. He had complained to Liz as they geared up. Didn't care that Maggie was standing right there.

'No one else is authorized to deploy except the rescue swimmer,' Wilson finally told her. 'We can send down anything she needs. Anything that might help her. But we stay in the helicopter. Or we have to leave and send a cutter back.'

'You'd leave her down there?'

More silence.

'Sometimes you don't have a choice. You follow the rules. I have a responsibility to the entire crew.'

'But the hurricane—'

'Exactly,' was his one-word answer. A pause, then, 'Seven minutes, Kesnick.'

'You can't just leave her.'

'Agent O'Dell, you do not have any authority in this craft. I do. Understand?'

'I don't see her,' Kesnick yelled.

'Give her a tug.'

'Nothing.'

They waited.

Maggie's heart pounded against her rib cage, the rhythm the same as the thump-thump of the rotors. Sweat rolled down her back and yet she felt chilled. She watched Wilson's profile. Jaw clamped tight. His visor prevented her from seeing his eyes, but his hands were steady, fists clenched on the control. Beside him, Ellis was an exact contrast – head bobbing and twisting around, trying to see below.

'This is the Coast Guard,' Ellis yelled into the radio. *'Restless Sole,* can you hear me?'

'Five minutes,' Wilson said. 'Where the hell is she?'

'Restless Sole, can you hear me?' Ellis shouted but only got static in response.

That's when it hit Maggie. *Restless Sole.* Wasn't that the name of Joe Black's boat?

'No one's answering,' Ellis said.

'Kesnick?'

'I don't see her.'

'We have got to get the hell out of here. Pull her up, Kesnick. PULL HER UP NOW.'

Kesnick obeyed. The cable whined and spun. Maggie waited to see Liz come over the doorway. Instead, she saw Kesnick grab the cable and spin around to his pilots. He didn't say a word as he held up the cable. It had been cut.

SIXTY-FIVE

Liz couldn't do a thing as the cable whipped away from her and flew out of the cabin. Her lifeline was gone.

But she wouldn't have left now anyway. Not without her dad.

She asked if she could bandage his hand. He held it up and against his chest, the front of his jumpsuit already drenched in blood.

'I'm okay, darling,' Walter insisted.

She recognized the woman from the beach. She had never seen the man who casually introduced himself as Joe Black, never letting the revolver slip from her temple.

'We'll just all stay put for a while and the helicopter will go away.' Joe didn't sound fazed.

'They won't leave their rescue swimmer,' Walter said.

Liz couldn't tell her dad that wasn't the way it always worked. It had happened once after Katrina. The helicopter had been dangerously low on fuel and packed with injured survivors. Liz had told them to go ahead while she waited on an apartment rooftop with a dozen others, angry and impatient for their turn. It was nightfall before her aircrew was able to return.

'I'll end up with three healthy specimens,' Joe continued to rant. 'I don't have enough ice but I suppose I could tether a couple of you to the back of the boat. Put life jackets on.'

'Specimens.' The woman spit it out like she was disgusted and certainly not afraid. 'You're gonna nickel-and-dime my body parts? Is that what you have in mind, young man?' She was holding her ankle but it didn't stop her. 'I'll have you know that my husband was murdered for millions of dollars. Millions.'

Joe Black ignored the woman. He stood, braced inside the stairwell, blocking their way but also able to keep an eye on all of them. He'd tethered himself to the railing and was able to ride out the boat's pitching back and forth. When Liz almost fell, the revolver swung down with her.

The boat rocked more violently, climbing and falling with the cresting waves. The noise was deafening. There was a crash somewhere up above them. Something had come down hard on the deck. Their eyes lifted to the ceiling. That's when they heard the helicopter rotors moving away. Within seconds the sound grew faint. They were leaving.

Liz's eyes met her dad's across the cabin. She knew her crew couldn't stay. A cutter would take forever to find them in these conditions. It probably wasn't even safe to try. This wouldn't be like her Katrina rooftop experience. This time her aircrew wouldn't return.

Joe Black was grinning.

'So who wants to go first?' he asked.

If Liz rushed him, he'd shoot her before she could get the gun away from him. What had she told Maggie O'Dell? It wasn't about being brave; it was about surviving. Fighting against crushing waves or dangling from a cable didn't scare her. Even when survivors challenged her, she'd count on her training, redirect her adrenaline. Maybe she could talk this guy off his ledge.

Joe Black pointed the gun at Liz as though he could hear her thoughts.

'A cutter's on its way,' she lied. 'The helicopter probably had it in sight. That's why they left.'

She saw him consider it. Something crashed above again, and his eyes shot up but only briefly. Another wave slammed the boat. There was a high-pitched screech of something skidding across the deck.

'The boat's being ripped apart,' the old woman yelled.

'Shut the hell up,' Black screamed at her, repositioning himself in the stairway and taking aim.

'NO.' She heard her dad yell, followed by the blast of a gunshot.

Liz closed her eyes against the pain, but there was no pain. When her eyes flew open she saw Joe Black fall forward, grabbing at his leg with one hand, the gun still in his other.

There was a shout from the top of the stairs. 'FBI. Drop it. Now.'

He hesitated.

Another shot chewed up the carpet next to him.

He threw the gun aside.

Liz stood paralyzed as Maggie climbed down the steps, her gun still pointed at Black.

'Liz, grab his weapon.'

She obeyed.

'Is he the only one?' Her eyes darted around the cabin and quickly returned to Black. When she glanced up for an answer, all Liz could manage was a nod.

'Everybody okay?' Maggie finally asked.

Liz heard the helicopter returning. All eyes lifted to the ceiling again.

'How did you–'

But Maggie interrupted her. 'We have to do this quickly.' Then to Liz she said, 'Wilson's in a pissy mood.'

THURSDAY, AUGUST 27

SIXTY-SIX

PENSACOLA, FLORIDA

Liz woke up as the last stream of sunset lit the room. She had slept hard. Her mouth was dry, her eyelids still heavy. It took a few seconds to remember where she was. Second floor. Her dad's house. Her old room had been made into a guest bedroom but there were still remnants of her childhood – a porcelain doll on the dresser, the embroidered pillow shams – and reminders of her mother.

She could hear chain saws down below despite the hum of the window air conditioner. Her dad had set up the unit especially for her, dropping a bright-orange electrical cord out her window, stringing it down the side of the house and along the backyard to the garage where he had it plugged into one of his generators. A definite luxury, since the window air conditioner took almost as many watts as one of his refrigerators.

'You deserve to sleep,' he had told her when she came home for the first time around noon. It was already in her bedroom window. She hadn't asked how he'd managed to put it

285

there with only one hand, his left one wrapped in a soft cast that made it look like he was wearing an oven mitt.

In the last two days Liz had napped for only a few hours at a time, rotating in barracks set up for them at NAS. The hurricane had lost some of its steam, winds dropping to 135 miles per hour as it made landfall. Its path had slipped to the east, sparing Pensacola the brunt of the storm. By the Saffir-Simpson Hurricane Wind Scale, a cat 4 meant 'devastating damage' but not 'catastrophic damage' like a cat 5.

Liz and her aircrew had rescued dozens of people from their flooded homes. Some still refused to leave, insisting they needed to stay and protect what belongings remained from looters. One man argued with Liz, refusing to leave his roof unless she allowed him to take four suitcases he had stuffed with valuables. By the end of the first day, Wilson no longer complained about sharing cabin space with an assortment of cats and dogs that accompanied their injured owners. And after having a madman almost shoot her, everything else seemed tame. But she'd bagged too many hours and now she was grounded.

Liz got up, pulled on a pair of shorts and a T-shirt. She glanced out the window, looking down over the street. Electrical wires still dangled from branches. Debris piles lined one side of the cul-de-sac where neighbors continued to drag and toss pieces of huge live oak trees, several of them uprooted. And in the middle of the street was the Coney Island Canteen. Lawn chairs were gathered around the mobile unit while her dad and Trish cooked dinner for their neighbors. He'd mentioned to Liz earlier that they were grilling steaks, burgers, hot dogs – even lamb chops – salvaging what they could from everyone's freezers. County officials were estimating the power being out for at least a week.

Liz could see him wiping the sweat from his forehead as he stood over the grill. She still couldn't shake that image of him holding his bloodied hand, the front of his jumpsuit soaked with blood. His face so pale. He'd spent the hurricane in the hospital, calling Trish to pick him up as soon as the main roads were cleared. From what Liz understood, Trish hadn't left his side.

Trish had refused to talk about Scott. All Liz knew was that he had spent the hurricane locked inside the funeral home's walk-in refrigerator. Liz had heard that Joe Black had left several corpses with Scott, and now he and the funeral home were under investigation.

As soon as Liz left her bedroom, the warm air hit her. She was damp with sweat by the time she joined her dad in the street.

'You didn't sleep very long, darling.'

'I'm hungry.'

'Well, sit yourself down. You came to the right place.'

The aroma of grilled meat and the spices her dad used overpowered the gasoline fumes from generators and chain saws. The sun was almost down. It would be pitch-dark in a couple of hours. Several neighbors were bringing out lanterns and setting them up for their evening meal in the street. The one advantage after a hurricane was that there were no mosquitoes, no bugs of any kind. But also no birds.

'Liz, you're just in time,' Trish said. 'Why don't you set up some plates and cups.'

'She needs to rest,' her dad said, surprising both of his daughters. Usually he let Trish boss Liz around. It was easier than getting in the middle. 'Ask Wendy to help.'

Trish stared at him for a minute before finally taking his advice.

'Have you heard anything from your FBI friend?' her dad asked.

'Just for a few minutes this morning when I was still at NAS. Otherwise, cell-phone towers are down.'

'She's one brave girl.' He pulled an ice-cold bottle of beer from the cooler at his feet and handed it to Liz. 'And so are you.'

288

SIXTY-SEVEN

JACKSONVILLE, FLORIDA

Maggie stopped her rental car at the security booth. She handed over her badge and waited while the guard picked up the phone. She lifted her arm to adjust the rearview mirror and a pain shot through her elbow. Actually, her entire body hurt. Who knew jumping from a helicopter could be so physically strenuous?

The guard passed back her badge.

'First building to your right. The others are waiting.'

Maggie'd gotten up early to catch footage of the storm damage. Charlie Wurth had told her earlier that Pensacola was lucky. At the last minute the storm had suddenly weakened and veered to the right. It made landfall as a category 4, but that was better than they expected. Watching the news reports, Maggie certainly didn't think Pensacola was lucky. The storm had still ripped apart roofs, blown out windows, and flooded homes. Electricity was out for more than a hundred thousand customers and not expected to be up and running for at least a week.

She had talked to Liz Bailey earlier, too, relieved to hear that Walter and Charlotte were okay. She was especially glad to hear that Walter would retain full use of his left hand, but it would take months of rehab. And despite sounding totally exhausted, Liz seemed to be handling the aftermath of the storm.

A military cargo plane flew low over Maggie's car, preparing to land. As she parked in front of the building she could feel the vibration. She eased out of the car and was grateful there was only a set of five steps. Ridiculous. She thought she was in good shape. She didn't like being reminded of dangling from that cable. Without effort she could conjure up the terror. She could hear the wind swirling around her and feel the rain pelting her face.

She needed some sleep, that's all. Last night she had dreamed of severed hands coming up out of the water and clinging to her. Okay, she needed dreamless sleep. Maybe another of Platt's massages. That brought a smile.

Inside, she had to show her badge again. A small woman in uniform led her down a hallway and into a conference room. Benjamin Platt was in uniform. She didn't recognize the other two men.

Platt did the introductions.

'Agent Maggie O'Dell, this is Captain Carl Ganz and Dr. Samuel McCleary.'

Dr. McCleary decided to open defensively. 'Joseph Norris has been a respected part of this program for almost ten years.'

Maggie could see Platt bristle.

'Then you understand, Dr. McCleary,' she began, 'that means you may have contaminated tissue and bone from as long ago as ten years.'

'All of our tissue is tested.'

'But only for certain diseases,' Platt said.

'No one could have predicted what happened at NAS in Pensacola,' McCleary insisted, shaking his head. 'That was one mistake. One out of thousands. And we've traced the grafts and bone paste Captain Ganz used. We think it all came from one donor.' He pointed to a document already set among a pile on the table. 'One donor who may have been dead longer than twelve hours.'

'Actually, it was more like twenty-one hours,' Platt said.

'We don't know that for certain.'

'He was dead long enough for his bowels to burst and *Clostridium sordellii* to start spreading to his tissue.'

'You have no proof of that,' McCleary said.

'What about the donors Joe Black obtained without certification?' Maggie asked.

'Joseph Norris,' McCleary corrected her, 'followed procedure as far as I am able to judge.'

'There's a funeral home in Pensacola,'

Maggie told him, 'that has two bodies. The Escambia County sheriff says both are homeless men who disappeared just days before the hurricane. The funeral director insists Joe Black brought them there and cut one of them up to be sold and used for educational conferences.'

This time McCleary was speechless.

'Joe Black was making a nice living on the side,' she continued. 'Diener by day, body broker during the weekends and on his days off. He admits to using soldiers' amputated parts when he came up short on an order. He already confessed that he used a few of your donors' bodies. The surgical conferences paid big bucks and he couldn't keep up with the demand.'

'You'll need to check our entire supply,' Ganz said to McCleary. 'Norris also admits to making substitutions, replacing healthy tissue with damaged tissue.'

Dr. McCleary nodded, an exaggerated bobbing of his head that told Maggie he would allow the possibility but didn't agree.

'Come,' he said, and he led them out of the room and down a long hallway. 'You want to do this, fine. I'll show you what you're in for.'

He slid a key card and waited for the security pad to blink green. He waved the three of them into a huge room that reminded Maggie of a police evidence room, only the shelves were replaced with drawers, one on top of another. Refrigerated and freezer drawers. Rows and rows.

'Would you like to start with the feet?' McCleary said, pointing at one end. 'Or perhaps the eyes?'

AUTHOR'S NOTE

I've spent most of my life in tornado country so I have a healthy respect for the forces of nature. In 2004 I bought what I believed would be a writing retreat just outside of Pensacola, Florida. Six months later, Hurricane Ivan roared ashore.

It's difficult to describe the damage and even more difficult to explain how deep the damage cuts beyond that to physical property. There's a transformation that takes place within the community. You spend long, hot days without running water and electricity. Gasoline and groceries are limited to what you've stocked before the storm. The clean up is physically and emotionally draining but you find yourself grateful to be working alongside neighbors, in my case, people I had only recently met. They taught me what true strength and perseverance looks like.

Nine months after Ivan, Hurricane Dennis made a direct hit. And the Pensacola community simply rolled up their collective sleeves and started cleaning up all over again.

To the community of Pensacola, please know that it was out of respect and admiration that I decided to use your piece of paradise as the backdrop of *Damaged*.

As in all my novels I blend fact with fiction. For the record, here are some of the facts and some of the fiction.

The premise of infecting an entire tissue bank is based solely on my speculation. There have been, however, fatal deaths caused by using infected donor tissue. One such case in 2001 found that a twenty-three-year-old man who died after routine knee surgery was killed by a rare bacterium – *Clostridium sordellii* – and that he contracted the infection from cadaver cartilage that was used to repair his knee.

Unlike organ donor banks, the standards for tissue, bone and other donated body parts are more loosely regulated. Even though the FDA established the HTTF (Human Tissue Task Force) in 2006, by their own admission, they continue to lack the resources to inspect and regulate this vast and growing industry.

The Uniform Anatomical Gift Act does prohibit the buying and selling of dead bodies, but the law does allow for companies to recover their costs for expenses such as labor, transportation, processing and storage. Demand is high, supply low, which sometimes gives way to fraudulent brokers such as the case of a New York funeral home where PVC pipe was swamped out for bones.

Yet, because of this industry, amazing technological advances have resulted. BIOmedics is fictitious, but similar companies have been creating and manufacturing innovative products like bone screws and bone paste, which have helped save the limbs of many soldiers returning from Afghanistan and Iraq.

It's true that the Naval Tissue Bank at the Naval Medical Center in Maryland was the first to use frozen bone transplants and to set up the first body donation program. However, to my knowledge you will not find a similar tissue bank in Jacksonville, Florida. Nor will you find Captain Ganz's surgical program at the Naval Air Station in Pensacola.

Likewise, I must offer my apologies to the Coast Guard's Air Station Mobile and Air Station Pensacola. I've taken a few liberties with take-offs and landings, many of which would not include Pensacola Beach.

While it is true that before Hurricane Dennis there were homemade signs asking the Weather Channel's Jim Cantore to 'stay away' or to 'go home,' I'm sure Mr Cantore has witnessed many similar signs in other communities. Hopefully he views these with the good nature they're intended as well as a tribute to his expertise.

And last, Charlie Wurth would have found

the Coffee Cup closed on Sundays, but if you're in Penascola any other day of the week, be sure to stop and try their award-winning Nassau grits.

ACKNOWLEDGEMENTS

Thank you to the men and women of the United States armed forces, especially the Coast Guard, for what you do every single day to keep us safe. And special thanks to those few women rescue swimmers for quietly and bravely shattering glass ceilings that most of us wouldn't dare attempt.

Thanks also to:

The incredible team at Doubleday – Jackeline Montalvo, Judy Jacoby, Alison Rich, Suzanne Herz, Lauren Lavelle, and John Pitts – for your warm welcome, your enthusiasm, dedication, and expertise.

Same goes to David Shelley, Catherine Burke and the crew at Little, Brown UK.

Amy Moore-Benson, my agent, for refusing to use the words 'never' or 'impossible'.

Lee Child, Steve Berry and Tess Gerritsen, three of the most generous authors in the business.

Ray Kunze, for lending his name to Maggie's boss. Just for the record, the real Ray Kunze is a gentleman and all-around nice guy who would never send Maggie into the eye of a hurricane.

Lee Dixon, for giving me the idea of identifying a torso by its defibrillator implant.

Darcy Lindner, funeral director, for sharing your expertise.

My friends – Sharon Car, Marlene Haney, Sandy Rockwood, Leigh Ann Retelsdorf, Patti and Martin Bremmer, and Patricia Sierra – for keeping me sane and grounded.

My family: Patricia Kava, Bob and Tracy Kava, Nancy and Jim Tworek, Kenny and Connie Kava, and Patti Carlin.

My Florida neighbors: Lee and Betty Dixon, Terry and Bea Hummel, Sharon and Steve Kator, Elaine and Kelly McDaniels, Lee and Carol McKinstry, Mike and Jana Nicholson, Steve and Anna Ratliff, Bill and Barb Schroeder, and Larry and Diane Wilbanks.

The booksellers, book buyers and librarians across the country, for mentioning and recommending my novels.

All you faithful readers – there's plenty of competition for your time, your entertainment, and your dollars. I thank you for continuing to choose my novels.

And, as always, special thanks to Deb Carlin, for everything. You are my Rock of Gibraltar.

Last, to Walter and Emilie Carlin. Walter passed away September 2008, and Emilie November 2005, but their enduring personalities, life stories, and spirit continue to inspire. Walter would have loved seeing his bright red, white, and blue Coney Island canteen come back to life, even if briefly and only in the pages of a novel.

The publishers hope that this book has given you enjoyable reading. Large Print Books are especially designed to be as easy to see and hold as possible. If you wish a complete list of our books please ask at your local library or write directly to:

Magna Large Print Books
Magna House, Long Preston,
Skipton, North Yorkshire.
BD23 4ND